THE DREAMERS

Insomnolence Book 2

D K CASSIDY

Pluvio
press

Editing: Crystal Watanabe

Cover: Artie Cabrera

ISBN: 978-1-941938-05-8

Library of Congress Control Number: 2017954016

Created with Vellum

ALSO BY D K CASSIDY

The Sleepless

To Mark, Aidan, Jared, Nikko,
Moongie, Bubble, and Mochi.

MAP OF THE NATION

CHAPTER ONE

President Glynis Grieves should have been happy.

Two weeks ago, she got the permission she'd been seeking for a decade. She finally had permission to euthanize the entire Sleepless population and shut down the Nation, so she could return to her life in Washington D.C. What was supposed to be a short-term assignment had turned into a decade of governing a useless group of citizens.

She looked at the copy of the speech she'd given, still stored in her tablet. Glynis reread her favorite part of that speech.

Before you consider how to word denying my request, let me explain one more thing to you. You will give me the permission I'm seeking this time. If, when I return tomorrow, my request has been denied, then I go public. I've documented everything about your great experiment and am prepared to release this information to the world. Imagine what will happen when all is revealed. You will be labeled monsters, and most, if not all of you, will be prosecuted for the use of illegal biological agents upon your own citizens.

Right before I stepped into this hearing, I was informed a group of Sleepers escaped from North City today and were last seen heading toward the Wall. Do you really want them to find out about all of this? I leave it to you to make the right decision. I'll be back in the morning to find out if you are indeed among the most intelligent men in the country or whether all these years of sitting on your behinds has only made you soft.

But as she'd learned over the course of her career, whenever something good happened, it seemed to be followed by something bad. She needed to concentrate on finding that group of Sleepers to be sure they weren't doing something that would ruin her plan.

Glynis shook her head, remembering how poorly she'd treated Remus. He'd said waiting to capture the group of Sleepers might end in a way that she hadn't wanted. Instead of listening to him, she took her time, and when her security squad showed up at the Sleepers' encampment, they were gone. They searched for a few hours, came back, and reported to her they could not find them.

Now this group was causing her a huge headache. Glynis wouldn't admit her judgment error to anyone else, but she knew her arrogance was coming back to bite her. She wasn't the type of person to dwell on her errors. Instead Glynis worked on how to fix them. She wouldn't quit until she got the Nation back in order and the Sleepers were caught. Then she could finally silence the lot of them.

She didn't want the government to change their minds. There might be resistance to her idea of euthanizing the citizens if there was a chance she'd accidentally kill those who could still sleep.

Now back at the Nation, President Grieves called a meeting of her best aides. She laughed inwardly, knowing she rarely took the advice of these men, but she liked to put on a show as if she wasn't the sole decision-maker. She made a mental note to add a woman to her group of aides, hoping that would result in her meetings being less irritating. No use letting the citizens think she was a dictator. She'd fired the irritating aide that was there the day she spoke to Remus. On this day, she was surrounded by the three who she considered the least annoying.

"I've summoned you here to help me decide what to do about those damn Sleepers. Just as I've gotten some fantastic news—more about that later—they put a wrench in the works for me. I found out they've left their encampment just outside the city. And no, before you ask, I didn't know they were there. They were last seen headed north toward the Wall. You may not know this, but there have been precautions taken so that anyone who's stupid enough to try to escape cannot do so. But... I'm wondering if any of the Sleepers have obtained information about our defenses."

Roger raised his hand and waited to be acknowledged by Glynis.

"Yes, yes, this isn't an elementary school, Roger," she said irritably. "What is it?"

"What are these defenses? I didn't know there were any. Why would we need defense since anything outside the Wall is a wasteland? Is there something I should know?"

President Grieves glared at him. His insipid stupidity and curiosity was all the confirmation she needed that killing her staff along with the Sleepless was the right decision. Debriefing them that they'd been living a lie for ten years was too much bother. The day she walked out of the Nation, she would be alone. That day couldn't come soon enough for her.

"That is not significant now. What's important is the reason I stated for gathering you here. I want opinions, not questions. Don't show me your ignorance or you won't be coming to any more of these meetings."

The three aides looked down at the table, not wanting to make eye contact. At last, one of them was brave enough to speak up.

"I think there's no way the Sleepers know anything about our defenses or about the way things are run here, President Grieves. So instead of worrying about that, perhaps we should focus on a plan to capture them. I know there was a failed attempt to get them earlier." He looked at her anxiously. "I don't mean it's your failure, not at all. I'm sure it was the security detail's fault, and they just didn't hustle enough or didn't make a big enough effort to look for this group. What if you send another group looking for them, but instead of heading north, what if you have them head north-east? In fact, what about two groups—one heading northeast and one heading southeast? That way you've got everything covered."

Glynis smiled, a rarity for her.

"I like that idea, Frank. I like that idea a lot. You've now been promoted to my top aide. Gareth, you're now number two. And as for you, Roger, for your idiotic question, you're just hanging on the edge of being number three."

The three men, each with a facial reaction to match their change of status, didn't speak, waiting for what came next.

"I need to find Remus. Which of you useless men will help me do this?"

The three aides looked at each other, trying to gauge whether they should volunteer for the task.

"President Grieves, I would be glad to help find this Rufus," said Gareth.

"You idiot! I said his name is Remus. But whatever. You want to do this? Then gather up some security guards and get Remus to me as soon as possible. Do this for me and you will regain your position as my number one aide."

President Grieves would never admit a mistake to anyone

but herself. And she knew that dismissing Remus might turn out to be the biggest error in judgment of her life. She needed to find him, and she needed to do it quickly. It made her nervous not knowing how to find the Sleepers and not knowing what they were up to.

"Our meeting is over."

"Bu-but, I thought you had good news?"

"My news is no longer fit for your ears. Everyone get out of here and leave me alone! I have work to do. And so should you."

The three aides scurried out and gently closed the door behind them. Glynis smiled for the second time that day, enjoying her power. Pulling out her tablet, she tapped a file that guaranteed the cooperation of the U.S. Government. It contained the notes from the experiment that had accidentally caused the Sleepless epidemic. She'd handed over the file when they gave her permission for the euthanasia project. This copy was her little secret. And her insurance.

Just in case.

CHAPTER TWO

Decker ran his fingers over the Wall, ready to climb it. After two weeks of hiking next to it, this was the first spot that seemed to have enough hand- and footholds for him to attempt to ascend the huge pile of garbage.

The combat boots that Jeremy and Aidan had stolen for him weren't flexible enough for climbing, so he pulled them off and dug into his backpack to retrieve his old pair of running shoes. Once he'd tied his shoes and put on gloves to protect his hands from the sharp objects mingled in with all the trash, Decker was ready to go. It felt good to wear his old shoes again. They reminded him of his carefree days BIB, before insomnolence began. A time when his most important decision was what type of paint to buy for one of his art projects and whether to go for a run.

All the Sleepers gathered around the base of the Wall to watch. If Decker could scale this mountain and see what, if anything, was on the other side, it would be a huge help for all of them. He could feel the tension of the group as they watched him prepare. Then the silence was broken by the sound of Marian's four children, who were laughing and running around. Not being able to have her own children, she'd adopted four children who got lost during the evacuation of her city. Before setting off, Decker gave one of his grins to the group to emphasize the confidence he had that he'd be able to do this.

Then, without further ceremony, he took the first step onto an old door. Reaching as far as he could above his head, Decker grabbed the end of a baseball bat sticking out between some tin cans and the handlebars of a tricycle. He stopped, then looked up, trying to figure out whether to keep going straight up or to move to the side. After spotting some better holds, he adjusted his route by shifting over to the right a bit and grabbed on to a shopping cart.

He continued this way for several minutes, finding garbage he could use to step on, then locating items he could grab, turning it into a methodical method of climbing. *This is all that remains of our life BIB,* he thought as he gazed at the variety of garbage in the Wall. He'd told Kate that he referred to this as the Garbage Wall Shopping Center. Prior to today, he'd only shopped as far up as his arms could reach. There was much more variety up here.

After a few more minutes of climbing, Decker found something of interest. It was an MP3 player. He grabbed it and stuffed it into his pants pocket. Kate would be surprised. She'd asked for one, and now he'd be able to give it to her. Ten years of listening to the same playlist on her old MP3 player was driving her crazy.

He got about halfway up before he knew it was time to stop. Looking up above him, about fifty feet away, were curved iron spikes that would prevent him from going any further. The spikes had barbed wire wrapped around them, forming an impenetrable barrier to the top of the garbage wall. He tried to contain his disappointment so the rest of the Sleepers wouldn't begin to worry. He was their leader and had promised them that he'd find other Sleepers. What he hadn't told them yet was that he was also looking for a way out of the Nation. He'd heard rumor of a door. The only other person that knew about that rumor was Kate. She wanted Decker to tell the rest of the group, but he didn't want to add an extra layer of hope to what might be a false rumor. Too much disappointment would make it more difficult to keep the group's morale up.

Decker began to climb down slowly, not looking down at his friends. He didn't want to see what he knew would be a sea of disappointed faces trying to look cheerful. When he got to the bottom, he jumped down the last four feet, turned around, and with a smile said, "Well, time for Plan B."

Claudia moved closer to Decker, a look of concern on her face. "What happened, Decker? We couldn't tell why you stopped climbing."

"From here the garbage blocks the view of the top half of the Wall. There's a barrier up there that I couldn't pass. There might be a way to rig something to get over it, but we don't have the right supplies. No worries. We'll keep going and try again. Let's set up camp here and rest. It's been a long day of hiking."

Claudia nodded, and the group began to disperse. Each Sleeper had their assigned chore when they camped. Decker enjoyed watching the group going about their business as if everything was normal. Within an hour, the tents were set up and food was simmering over the campfire. He'd learned how to build low-smoke fires to prevent detection and had passed on that trick. Decker's father, during one of the rare times they'd gone camping, had taught him how. His father wasn't an outdoorsy type of man, but he'd wanted to test his latest toy, Swedish fire steel, a Father's Day gift from Decker. After researching various methods, they'd determined the one that worked best and stuck with it.

Being camped next to the Wall gave the rest of the group a chance to explore it. The children made attempts to climb as Marian looked on. One of them found an old doll and ran to Decker, excited about her find.

"Decker, Decker! Look at this!" Caroline skipped to him, waving the doll.

"That's a cool doll, Caroline."

"Can I keep it? Puh-leeze?"

Marian, watching their interaction, nodded at Decker.

"Yeah, why not? Are you going to give it a name?"

Caroline furled her four-year-old brow, concentrating on this important task.

"Trevor. That's what I'm gonna call it. Trevor. 'Cause it is going to be the king of all the dolls my mamma makes."

Decker watched the children's carefree play and smiled sadly. He wished he could feel that way again.

Late in the evening, all the Sleepers except for the children gathered around the campfire. No one talked. Instead, they stared at the Wall. Decker could tell they were wondering what was on the other side.

"What if we don't find any of the others?" said Claudia.

"I refuse to think that way," said Decker as he shook his head. "We know they're out there somewhere because Bridget lived with them. We'll keep going until we find them. From what she's told me, their encampment is permanent. The group hasn't moved in ten years. The other Sleepers she found were more transient, but that doesn't mean we can't track them down."

Stephen, who'd been quiet while the others were talking, asked a question. "Don't any of you ever wonder why we sleep? It seems so random. We're a group of various ages and races. Male and female. I just don't understand why we were so lucky."

Decker often had those thoughts but never brought it up with the group. He thought this was as good a time as any.

"You know what, Stephen? I think about that almost every day. On the surface, there doesn't seem to be any reason why we should sleep. I look at Kate and Aidan, and I wonder, how are they different from us? But I'm not a scientist; I'm an artist, so I'd probably be the wrong person to come up with something that makes sense. Maybe Jeremy can help us figure this out—he's more of a left-brain person. You up for that, Jeremy?"

Jeremy look surprised to be singled out and nodded his head.

"Okay, great, then. Maybe we could think of some questions together right now? Then Jeremy could come up with some sort of theory that will help us pin down the differences between us and Aidan and Kate. Let's go around the campfire, and each one of us can think of a question. Claudia, do you want to go first?"

"Well, like Stephen said, we know it's not about being male or female," said Claudia, "so we can rule that out. Let's start with lifestyle. Anyone here a vegetarian BIB? I know we all eat meat now, but I don't know what your eating habits were like in the past."

One person raised their hand. It was Marian. That knocked off vegetarianism.

"Okay, how about you, Aidan?"

"Well, did any of you take vitamins?" he asked. "I know it sounds kind of like a lame question, but I think that we probably have to think about everything no matter how insignificant it sounds."

This time three people raised their hands, including Aidan.

"Well, that was easy," said Decker. "Now we know that being a vegetarian or taking vitamins isn't the answer. Stephen, since you started this discussion, what do you want to ask?"

"How about we get more into our biology than our lifestyle? Have any of you ever had a vaccination for any reason?"

Everyone raised their hand.

"Hey," said Decker. "What about this? Have any of you traveled outside of the United States?"

Everyone, Sleepers and the Sleepless, raised their hands.

"Okay," said Decker, nodding. "I think before we go any further, we need to be writing these down and making a tally of the answers. On the face of it, it seems that none of these questions matter, but it could also be a combination of factors. As I said, I'm not a scientist, so I leave all that data stuff to Jeremy."

"I need to find some way to record the data," said Jeremy. "None of us have tablets. Anybody up for a shopping trip in town?"

No one volunteered.

"There is the old-fashioned method of writing on paper," said Decker. "Is there any left? I know our supply was getting pretty low."

"I know how to make paper," said Bridget. "I can make all you need."

"Ah, a woman of many talents," Decker said with a smile. "Okay, what do you need?"

"I'll help you, Bridget," said Kate. "I remember making paper with you when I was a little girl. That way we can have extra, so Decker and Claudia can draw." She looked over at them. "You've both been missing your art; I want to help you out."

The group agreed. Decker and Claudia smiled at the generous offer.

With the mood being so good, Decker made a decision. "Kate's been urging me to tell all of you about a rumor I heard." He paused. "There's a possibility that a door exists."

"What do you mean a door?" Claudia asked.

"A door located somewhere in the Wall. One that leads to the outside."

"But why would we want to go outside?" asked Stephen. "There's nothing there, and it's supposed to be dangerous."

"Let's not believe everything we've been told by the government until we find proof," said Decker. "First let's get up the Wall and see what's on the other side. If it's safe, we'll look for the door and other Sleepers."

Kate smiled at Decker. He knew she was happy he'd finally shared the rumor of the door with the rest of them.

Her smile gave him the courage to keep going. "I have another idea. We refer to ourselves as Sleepers. But does that describe who we really are? Right now we're on a quest to find other Sleepers, a reason for sleeplessness, and a way to escape the Nation. That doesn't sound like a bunch of people who just so happen to still sleep. We have big dreams. I'd like to start calling our group the Dreamers."

Everyone looked excited and nodded in agreement with him.

"Then it's decided. Goodnight, Dreamers. I'll see you in the morning."

A loud grunt made them all turn toward the Wall.

"Yeah, don't mind me. I'm only the *Dreamers'* dog," Remus said mockingly. "What're you all staring at? You're the ones that tied me up."

Remus began tugging at the rope around his neck. There wasn't enough slack for him to stand, as the end of his restraint was tied to a dilapidated refrigerator.

"Who cares what I think about the subject. Go on, treat me like an animal and continue to have your *intellectual* conversation. I'm all ears. Forget that you are no better than me." He spat. "No. You know what? You're worse than me. I'd never tie up a human and lead him around like a dog. You better hope I never get this rope off. Start sleeping with one eye open."

Decker frowned and motioned for everyone to disperse.

Stephen walked away without another word. Remus watched him go, confident he could turn him into an ally. Of all the Sleepers, that kid seemed the most malleable. Whenever the group discussed anything, Stephen seemed eager to agree. He'd even agreed to that stupid idea of calling themselves Dreamers. As if any of their dreams would come true. This was real life, not dreamland.

Remus knew the type. Stephen had no opinions of his own. Or he didn't have the nerve to express any.

He's such a wimp, but I'll make use of that. Oh, yes, I will.

He was sick of being treated like a prisoner. If only they knew how much trouble he could make for them. In truth, though, the source of his hatred was envy. They slept; he couldn't. It was as simple as that. Remus wasn't a complicated man; his needs and desires were primal. Food, sex, and someday the ability to sleep naturally. That was all he wanted. He'd hoped they'd reveal the secret of why they could sleep, but after hearing today's conversation, he was disappointed to learn they were clueless. Useless.

It was time for him to escape.

CHAPTER THREE

Dinner was cooking over the campfire. Vegetable soup flavored with dried herbs. It wasn't fancy, but it was healthy. The smell made everyone's mouth water except for one person. Kate was tired of eating soup.

"Could go for some fresh meat, Decker," said Kate. "I know it's only been a couple of weeks, but these EnUR-G bars are getting old and vegetable soup doesn't fill me up. You'd think I'd be used to their bland taste after ten years, but after eating the delicious stuff your group cooks, I'm having a hard time not craving other flavors."

"You could go hunt for something. I think it's your turn anyway." Decker turned and motioned toward Aidan. "Take Aidan with you."

Aidan tried not to panic. He hadn't killed anything since ... he couldn't even think about it. The nightmares were starting to wane, and this hunt might make them more frequent. But, not wanting to disappoint Decker, he took a deep breath and stepped forward.

"Yeah, sure, but I gotta warn you, I've never been hunting. City boy, remember?"

The three of them laughed, recalling the trouble Aidan had trying to identify fruit and vegetable seeds when he'd been assigned a test before he could join their group. Jeremy had gone along to help him steal the right seeds and to make sure he didn't run away.

Ten minutes later, Aidan and Kate were walking through the woods in amicable silence. He was deep in his thoughts, trying to figure out whether he could go through with the hunt. Suppressed memories had nearly surfaced already. And then, without warning, it happened. Ling's face appeared before him, a memory from her last minutes before he killed her during the Sector Series. He gasped and fell to his knees.

Kate put a hand on his shoulder. "What's wrong? Aidan, are you okay?"

Aidan shook his head, unable to speak for a moment. Kate sat next to him and hugged him and waited until he calmed down.

Kate pulled away and looked at him. "What is it, Aidan? Tell me, what is it?"

Aidan separated himself from Kate, more composed now. "I don't think I can help you with this hunt. I just saw Ling's death face. The way she looked at me as I was plunging the sword into her heart. Her ... her face haunts me at night. This is the first time in a while that I've seen it during the day. I'm not over the Sector Series, and despite Jeremy trying to help me through my feelings about this, my guilt won't go away."

Kate's face fell as she realized what he was going through, but she said nothing; she just listened.

"If I'm being honest with myself, I hope the guilt never goes away. Not wanting to do the wrong thing in the name of my sector, killing just for some stupid glory ... it's important to me. It should be important to any decent person. I'll never blindly follow orders again. From anyone or any country. Killing Ling and Jordan will stay with me for the rest of my life, and because of that, I don't think I can help you hunt." He looked at her sheepishly. "I know hunting animals is not the same, but the act of killing—I can't do it again."

"Oh, Aidan," said Kate, "I didn't even think about that when we asked you to hunt. You should have told me then. Of course you don't have to hunt. Do you want to go back? I can do this myself."

Aidan shook his head. "I'm not going to leave you alone. What if one of President Grieves's patrols is out here?" He stood up. "I'll come with you. I can't do the actual hunting, but I'll be by your side the whole way."

"You sure?" she asked.

Aidan nodded. "Don't worry, Kate, if I have to kill to protect you, I won't hesitate, but if I have a choice, like today, then the answer has to be no."

Kate got up as well, dusting off her hands. "Sounds like a plan. And I appreciate that you're willing to protect me. Just let me know if you need to stop or if you change your mind." She looked around. "Let's go farther into the woods and see what's around. Maybe we can find some mushrooms or berries. I'm so hungry for something fresh I could murder a tree and eat it right now."

They both burst out laughing.

They walked through the woods, keeping their eyes on the ground, looking for something for Kate to catch. He was impressed that she was relying on her quickness rather than weapons to catch an animal. Kate had a basket with her and was planning on using it to trap a small animal if she was unsuccessful catching anything with her hands.

Aidan stopped short and snapped his fingers softly. "Over there, Kate," he whispered. "There's a rabbit munching on some clover. You could sneak up on it."

"Shh. Don't move, Aidan."

Kate walked slowly toward the rabbit, trying to gauge

when to pounce. Patience was not a trait she possessed, so waiting was hard. She moved a few more inches, getting closer. Then she grabbed for the rabbit's ears, snatching—nothing. She could hear Aidan laughing behind her.

"Uh, show a little respect to your elders."

"Sorry, but you looked pretty funny when you brought your hand up and it was empty!"

"Yeah, well, maybe you should try it. How about you catch the bunny, and I whack it? Deal?"

"What do I get if I catch one?"

"Bragging rights. And dinner. Now you try it, funny guy."

Aidan wanted a distraction from his thoughts, so it sounded like a good challenge. He thought about how to do it, then remembered a game he'd played with his father BIB, when currency was still used. Aidan held his hand in front of himself, forming a U shape. His father would then hold a dollar bill between Aidan's fingers and without warning, let the bill drop. At first Aidan missed every time, but once he focused, he could catch it. He just needed to use the same mindset for this.

He spotted another rabbit eating ten feet away. Aidan stepped with care toward the animal until he was within arm's reach. Holding his breath, he stretched his arm toward the ears and closed his hands around ... nothing.

He heard Kate laughing behind him.

"Okay, it's harder than I thought. Let's try something else. Any ideas, Kate?"

"Let me stop laughing first."

Aidan rolled his eyes, then began laughing, too. "Who knew hunting could be so funny?"

Kate unrolled the wire she'd been carrying and began to set up a snare. She'd found the wire in the garbage wall and had been saving it for this. If successful, it would be the first time for Kate. She knew what to do in theory, but she had never practiced.

"Aidan, find me two sticks. A thin twig and a small branch."

Once she got what she needed, Kate stuck the two pieces of wood in the ground and tied one end of the wire to the branch. The other side of the wire she fashioned into a noose, then hung it from the twig. Something didn't look right, but it was close to what she thought it should look like.

"Now we wait," said Kate, and she ushered Aidan farther back into some bushes nearby.

A rabbit cautiously approached the snare, sniffing. Its head went up as if trying to determine if the smell from the snare belonged to something nearby. It circled around it, then hopped away. The snare remained intact.

After the failure with the snare, Aidan thought they should just go back and grab a bow and arrow or a knife to help with the hunt. He'd already begun to walk out of the woods when Kate called to him.

"Where are you going?"

He turned back to her with a quizzical look on his face. "Well, there's nothing else to try, is there? I think we're better off going back and having something else to help us."

"Boy, are you wrong, my young friend. There's one more idea I'd like us to try before we give up. I read about this a long time ago, and it's something I've always wanted to put into practice."

"What is it?" asked Aidan.

"It's called the tiger trap. What we do is dig a hole and then put some sticks and leaves on top, and then sit back and wait until a rabbit or squirrel or some sort of small animal steps on top of it. Then boom! They fall through and we have our dinner."

Aidan scrunched up his face. "That's it? Just a hole?"

"Actually, there should be sharpened spikes in there, too, so maybe we'll do that as well. I have a little penknife in my pocket. First we've gotta find a good spot. The rabbits seem to gather near the base of the trees, so let's build one of those traps near there. The ground should be soft enough if we avoid the roots."

Once Kate was finished describing the trap, Aidan tried to hide the trembling in his body. He'd never told her about the last moments of his fight with Ling and the fact that she'd made a modified tiger trap to hide herself. It was too much for him and he couldn't hold back. He covered his face with his hands and began to scream.

"What is going on? Stop screaming and calm down, Aidan. Was it something I said?"

Kate ran over to Aidan and grabbed him, trying to calm them down, but it didn't work; he continued to scream and shake. And all he could say over and over again was, "No no no no."

"Aidan, come on, tell me. What is it? What did I do?"

Still shaking, he sat down with his head between his knees and then began to sob. Kate left him alone, waiting until he could gather himself. After five full minutes, he stopped but remained in a crouched-over position.

"Do you want to talk now?"

Aidan sat up with red teary eyes and a blotched face and nodded to Kate.

"There's no way you would've known this, but when I had to fight Ling, she built a modified tiger trap. She was waiting in that trap with her spear, ready to impale me. That's where I saw her face as I stabbed her. That calm look on Ling's face ... I don't know how I'll ever forget that."

"That's it. You're never coming on another hunting trip again. We need to go back and get you calmed down. Maybe Bridget can make you some soup. There are a lot of other things you can do for us, but I will never ever ask you to come hunting again. And if at some point later you ask to come, I'm going to make sure you truly mean it and aren't offering out of obligation. Agreed?"

All Aidan could do was nod. They walked back to the camp without any meat for dinner. Bridget was standing at the edge of the camp waiting for them.

"Oh, honey, you look terrible. Come with me and I'll make you something to eat, okay?"

Aidan nodded and followed Bridget to her tent.

He felt comforted by Bridget; she reminded him of his grandmother. The big difference, though, was that he couldn't imagine his grandmother hiking around for years on her own and being so self-sufficient.

"Okay, Aidan, I want you to lie down inside your tent, crawl under your covers, and wait for me to bring back some soup. All right?"

Aidan nodded, and he headed for his tent and flopped down on his blanket. He began to feel drowsy, his eyelids becoming heavier. Just as he was about to drop off, he snapped back awake. He'd almost *fallen asleep*. Could adrenaline cure his sleepless state? Then he realized being in a heightened state of fear or shock would be worse than not being able to sleep.

Bridget returned with a huge bowl of nettle soup.

"Aidan, sit up a little and eat this soup. It will calm you down. There are properties in nettles that will be good for you."

"How do you know so much about these things, Bridget?"

"I knew a lot about this BIB, and over the last ten years, I've done some experimentation and found plants that work. Don't ever ask me to cook up any mushroom soup, though. Even though I love mushrooms, I stay away from those because I can't always tell the difference between the good ones and the poisonous ones."

Bridget laughed, and after a moment, Aidan did, too.

"Do you want to talk about what happened, Aidan? I'm a good listener."

"I can't. Ask Kate about it; she'll fill you in. I just want to put it behind me. This soup is delicious, by the way. I'm feeling much better. Maybe I should get out of bed now. I feel like a baby for losing it out there."

"You should be proud of yourself for being able to express your feelings," said Bridget. "No one will fault you for that. But if you want to get up, come with me to pick some herbs. I'll teach you what to look for."

"I'd like that. My seed-stealing stint made me aware of my interest in plants. Before that day, I never noticed them other than as part of the scenery. Maybe you can teach me about the medicinal properties. We could become the group healers."

She patted his hand warmly and smiled. "Wouldn't that be nice?"

CHAPTER FOUR

Remus was mad. After over two weeks of being with the Dreamers, he was still tied up and being led around by a rope. He felt like a dog. The degradation of being treated as less than human was wearing on him. He'd hoped that after the first few days the group would learn to trust him and untie him. But he now knew this wasn't going to happen. He also knew that his behavior and habit of talking back to everyone wasn't helping his case. He blamed his sorry condition on the leader, Decker.

I need a plan. Can't stand to be treated like an animal. But I need an ally.

When he'd spied on this group, he'd heard Stephen's misgivings about allowing Kate to join them. Could he use that to befriend Stephen? He didn't have another plan, but he wasn't sure where they were and thought he was probably always being watched, so sneaking off alone wasn't going to work. Remus needed help. When they settled down that evening, he knew it was time for him to take some sort of action.

"Uh, you there. Kid."

Stephen looked over at Remus, apparently unsure if he was the one being addressed. Then he saw Remus motioning him over. Remus knew Stephen would be wary of him and think he was trying to trick him. He'd been warned about him by Decker; they all had. But Remus had heard Stephen complaining about being his guard every afternoon.

"What? I just fed you. Need to piss?"

"Nothing like that. Wanted to talk. I'm bored. What was your name again?"

"Am I supposed to feel sorry for you? My name is Stephen, the same name I told you about twenty times. Problems with your memory, old man?"

"Yeah, funny, funny. Poke fun at the old guy. Next you and your kind will have me eating my food on my hands and knees out of a bowl like some stupid mutt. That'll make you happy, huh?"

Stephen frowned, clearly bothered by Remus's statement.

Remus rejoiced inwardly. *So this kid feels bad about the way they're treating me. This could be useful.*

"You think you could loosen the rope around my neck? It's chafing. If you look you can see the redness."

Stephen sighed heavily. "I've been warned repeatedly to be careful of you, so don't try to escape. But I'll look at that rope. I can probably loosen it a bit for you." Stephen looked around to see if anyone was watching. Then he got closer to Remus and inspected his neck.

Remus watched Stephen's face while he was examining the knot on the rope, trying to read whether he could get any sympathy from him.

"Well, it does look a little tight," Stephen said, his brow furrowing. "Just hold still and stop wiggling for a bit. If you try anything, I'm going to yell for Decker and Jeremy. They'll be here in a second, so don't try anything. Got it?"

Remus nodded meekly.

Stephen fiddled with the rope a bit. "That any better?"

Remus nodded again and attempted a smile, showing his pointy, ratlike teeth.

"So, kid—I mean, Stephen, how long you been with this group?"

"Why are you suddenly interested in me?" He narrowed his eyes at Remus. "We've barely muttered more than a handful of words to each other over the past couple of weeks. You never found it necessary to have a conversation with me. Other than 'I'm hungry' or 'I gotta take a leak.' Do you really think I'm that stupid?"

Remus could read the suspicion and skepticism on Stephen's face. He knew he had to tread lightly. "No. I just want to be treated like a human, that's all. Thought maybe you'd be nicer than some of the other jerks who've been dragging me along. But, hey, go away if you want. It doesn't matter to me."

Stephen's shoulders slumped a little, and Remus noticed the slight look of guilt on his face. "Nah, I'll talk to you. Done all my chores for today, so I have some time." He paused. "If you really want to make friends with me, tell me about you, Remus. Prove to me this isn't a trick."

This is an interesting development.

"Do you want to know about my life AIB or BIB? How much time you got?"

"Well, I'm not on cooking duty tonight, so go for it. Start with where you were born, Remus."

Stephen sat on a dilapidated metal chair next to the refrigerator Remus was tied to.

"The place of my birth?" Remus laughed. "I was born in Kansas. It's flat as far as the eye can see. Not much to do, so I hated the place. How about you, Stephen? Where did you begin your life?"

"I was born in Chicago and lived there my entire life BIB.

It's also flat, but we have Lake Michigan. The lake is so huge it feels like an ocean."

"Lucky you. I always wanted to see the Pacific or the Atlantic Ocean. But living next to Lake Michigan would be a good second choice. Hey, do you happen to have any extra food on you? I could use a little snack, kid."

Stephen rustled around in his pockets and pulled out an EnUR-G bar. Holding it up, he offered it to Remus.

"Yummy," said Remus sarcastically. "That's exactly what I wanted. Thanks anyway, but I'd rather munch on some dirt."

"I can help you out with that." Stephen offered Remus a handful of dirt. "Here you go. Let me know how this tastes."

Remus laughed. "Okay, point taken, kid. You got a sense of humor; I like that. Lemme have that bar. I really am hungry."

When Remus finished eating, he continued with his little autobiography.

"I was an only child. We lived on a farm in the middle of effing nowhere. When my father wasn't farming, he was drinking or beating up my mom. Think the only reason he never beat me up is because he was too tired after a full day's work. My mother, though, she was the nice one, and the best thing that ever happened to me. But after watching my father beat her up for a few years, I ran away at fourteen."

Remus could tell he was getting to Stephen. His powers of persuasion hadn't been affected by his imprisonment.

"Yeah, I ran away to the big city of Wichita. I got pulled into some pretty nasty stuff while I was there. You don't want to hear about it, though; you'd be shocked."

Stephen shook his head, just as Remus expected he would.

"And after that, nothing much exciting happened to me. Got addicted to heroin, robbed a few convenience stores, and wound up spending some time in jail. So yeah, I haven't had a great life. Kind of explains why I'm such an ass right now. I mean, everything was against me."

Remus checked Stephen's face again for his reaction and could see this kid was really a sucker. None of that stuff had happened to him. He'd had a normal childhood, and the only reason he was a jerk was because it was fun. He knew he was probably a psychopath but wasn't gonna let on about his suspicion.

"I don't know what to say about your life, Remus. That's all just so sad. As for me, I had a nice life, but now I feel guilty about it. Both my parents loved me. I have a brother and sister, although I don't know where they are right now. Don't know if my parents are still alive, either. We got separated during the evacuations AIB. I never had to worry about where my next meal was coming from and was never in fear of getting hit. My parents didn't even spank me. Your life explains a lot about you, Remus."

Remus resisted the urge to smile at how gullible Stephen was.

"It's okay, kid. Not everyone had a crappy life like me. It could've been worse. What if I'd turned into a serial killer or something, right?"

"Yeah, that's true, but your life BIB, all of it, sounds so horrible," said Stephen.

"I *did* like to torture animals. Skin them alive."

"*What?*"

Remus saw the look of shock on Stephen's face and decided he'd better tone it down. "It's a joke, kid, calm down. Enough about the past, I need to keep thinking about the future."

"Have you thought about turning your life around and doing some good for others?" asked Stephen. "That might help you feel better about yourself. Maybe you could assist us somehow. Like telling us more about the president and what's going on in the Capital? Or tell us the secret of why we sleep and you don't."

Remus fumed inwardly. He hated to be lectured, and he especially resented it coming from a kid.

"Hold on, Mr. Goody Two-shoes. Who said I feel bad about myself? And don't rub in the whole 'you can sleep and I can't' shit. I don't know anything about that. You're hurting my feelings."

"I'm sorry, I just assumed—"

Remus laughed. "Nah, it's all good. You're probably too nice to hurt anyone's feelings. I get the feeling you've never done anything mean in your life."

Stephen's face turned slightly red at that, but Remus didn't like the direction the conversation was going. He had to steer it back to his plan; then he realized the potential of his new subject.

"I don't know anything about the Nation's plans. I was just a thug for President Grieves. You know, doer of the dirty work. Rough people up, that kinda thing. Nope, the only way I'm going to be able to redeem myself is to go back to her and tell her I'm still loyal to her and the government. She'll believe me. She said I was her most trusted thug."

"Bu—"

Remus held up his grimy hand to stop Stephen from talking. *Man, it's fun to lie to this stupid kid.* "Before you say anything, I know that sounds wrong, but if I were captured right now, I'd be executed as a traitor. And by executed, I mean I wouldn't be allowed access to Somnum. Dying of sleep deprivation is a horrible way to go, kid. Better if I go back and pretend to still be a loyalist. That way, once I get back into her good graces, she'll tell me something that I can pass on to the Sleepers. What do you think about that, Stephen?"

Stephen didn't look convinced. "Don't forget, we call

ourselves Dreamers now. I like it, and I want you to refer to us that way, okay? Anyway, on the surface your plan makes sense. But how would you get back to the Capital? You can't escape. Everyone's watching you all the time."

And this is where I set the trap. "Not without help. And there is someone who can help me," said Remus, looking directly at Stephen.

Stephen looked at him blankly for a couple of seconds. "Oh no! You don't mean me, right? I don't break rules. I've never broken a law, plus I love this group. Give me a good reason why I would help you escape, and by doing so, betray Decker, Kate, and everyone else? I couldn't live with myself."

"You got it all wrong, kid. You wouldn't be betraying the Dreamers; you'd be helping them. If you get me out of here and come along with me, I can introduce you to the president. Nice woman. Did I tell you she lets me call her Glynis? Maybe get you a job in the Capital. You're good at pretending, aren't you?"

Stephen looked wary but nodded.

"Between the two of us, we could both find out some useful information for the Dreamers. I'm only doing this to help you out, kid. You've been nice to me. There's no good reason for me to go back to that city. Even though your group treats me like a dog"—he rattled his chain for emphasis— "I appreciate the fact you didn't kill me back at your camp. It sure would've been easier. I still don't understand why I'm alive."

The best thing now was to be quiet and let Stephen mull over everything he just heard, so instead of speaking, Remus looked toward the encampment, his resentment growing. Silence for a few minutes. Then Stephen looked like he made his mind up about something.

"This plan of yours goes against everything I've ever been

taught. But I admit, what you say seems to make sense. I'll help you on two conditions."

"Yeah? What are they?" asked Remus.

"That we don't hurt anyone when we escape. You hurt someone, and I'll help them catch you and tell them all about your plans. This is the only way I'll help you."

"Of course. I won't hurt any of your friends. The whole point of this plan is to help them, Stephen. What's the second condition?"

Stephen smiled. "Stop calling me kid. I'm a man, and you're only about ten years older than me. We're partners now, so show me some respect."

"You got it, ki—I mean, Stephen. So we're good on this plan to escape together?"

"I'm not escaping, you are. But yes, I will help you leave here to get back to the city. We'll do the best we can to help not only my Dreamers, but the other Sleepers that we know are out there."

And the trap was sprung.

CHAPTER FIVE

Remus and Steven chose to leave the Dreamers' encampment after midnight, when everyone would be asleep. There was someone on watch every night, so they chose an escape route that avoided that part of the camp. Stephen went to where Remus was being held and greeted him by lifting two backpacks. Remus had to fight the urge to laugh.

"Did you get something to cut this rope off me?"

Stephen dug into one of the backpacks and pulled out a hunting knife and began to saw at the ropes. First the one around Remus's neck, and then the ropes tied tightly around his wrist.

"There you go. You're a free man now," said Stephen.

"The backpack's for me? If so, hand it over, kid. Damn, sorry. I gotta get used to calling you by your name. Hand it over, please, *Stephen*."

"You can look inside if you want to. I packed yours with the same stuff as I have in mine. You want to go through it or just get going?"

Remus hesitated for a moment because he wanted to be

sure they had enough to survive the trip back to the Capital, but he knew that they couldn't afford to waste time.

"Nah, I trust you. If you didn't pack well, then we'll both die out there. Happy thought, right?"

They walked quietly past the camp, neither one of them speaking, concentrating on not rustling leaves or snapping branches. When they were a mile away, they began to pick up the pace. At that point, it didn't matter if they made a little noise. Remus looked over at Stephen to see if he had any second thoughts about their escape. From what he could tell, Stephen looked like he was concentrating on being quiet, but he didn't think he looked conflicted. Remus didn't really know what conflicted looked like; he was never conflicted about anything, but he figured Stephen had come this far, and that had to count for something.

"How far do you intend to go tonight, Remus? Are you fit enough to go the entire way in by walking all night, or should we camp somewhere?"

Remus bristled at the insinuation that he was a tired old man, even though he was. "Let's just go for another hour or so, and then I think we should find a place to sleep because we don't want to show up at President Grieves's office looking exhausted, dirty, and bedraggled. In fact, let's see if we can find someplace near a spring so we can take a bath."

Stephen look surprised at the mention of a bath, as if his current state was how dirty Remus always was. Then Remus realized Stephen had never seen him in any other condition and probably assumed he was just slovenly in general. The day the Dreamers captured him, he'd rubbed dirt on his face and arms as a form of camouflage.

"Try not to look too surprised, kid. I clean up pretty well," said Remus.

It was another hour before they found a place that could serve a dual purpose for them: to bathe and spend the night, secure from the eyes of the Dreamers, who by now would be looking for them. There was a deep stream that flowed past a circle of trees. Looking inside the circle, Remus saw a thick layer of moss. He also noticed that unless someone came into the circle, they would not be able to see them resting there. Stephen came up behind him.

"Hey, Remus, this is definitely the place for us to stay."

"Yup. Good thing, 'cause I gotta admit, I'm pretty beat. You wanna bathe first? I'll look around for some firewood. You know how to build a fire, kid?"

"I, Stephen, not *kid*, do know how to build a fire. And yeah, I feel filthy, so sure, I'll go first. I'll let you know when I'm finished."

Remus wandered around looking for sticks and twigs that Stephen could use to start a fire. The main reason he wanted Stephen to take the first bath was he needed to decide. Should he leave the kid behind? After all, he'd helped him escape already. Why did he need to keep him around? Or would he be better off bringing Stephen to the Capital as his prisoner to prove that he did know where the Sleepers were located? A glimmering of conscience tried to break through, but Remus suppressed it. He didn't want to anger President Grieves. He knew it was her fault she didn't start searching sooner for the Sleepers, but he was also aware that she was the type of woman to blame everyone but herself. He decided to stick around for now.

Stephen went about setting up a fire while Remus headed to the stream. He had a dirty soul but liked to keep his body clean, and it had been so long since he'd had one that he let out an immense sigh when he entered the water. He floated and stared at the sky, fantasizing about all the accolades he would get upon his triumphant return to the Capital. Once he'd washed and scraped off all the dirt and filth from his body, he returned to a roaring campfire.

"You do know how to make a fire," said Remus. "Now, how about hunting? You any good at it?"

"I guess."

"Good," said Remus. "'Cause I'm not. Never had to hunt before."

They both slept soundly after a feast of rabbit and water. The next morning, they continued their journey. Before falling asleep, Remus decided he had to use Stephen as a pawn in his plan to curry President Grieves's favor. Poor naïve Stephen had no idea he was walking into a trap.

They entered the North City outer border, then moved on to the ITS station. Jumping the turnstile, they found the express train to the Capital.

"There it is, Stephen, the Capital. Have you ever seen it?"

"No, I've only been in North City. There was never a reason for me to come to the Capital, especially after I left North City to join the Dreamers."

"We'll be in front of the president within the hour. I think you'll enjoy meeting her," said Remus.

The imposing entry to the Capitol Building was a familiar site that made Remus glad he'd returned. It felt like it was greeting the returning hero. Before he entered, he turned to Stephen and told him not to talk, to just follow him. Remus promised to take care of everything.

"I need to speak to President Grieves at once!"

The startled aide looked up from his tablet.

"Do you have an invitation or an appointment? What is your name?" asked Roger, President Grieves recently demoted aide.

"I don't need an appointment. My name is Remus. That's

all you have to tell her. She will want to see me. And tell her I've brought a gift."

"You can't demand to see her. Go away."

"If she hears you've prevented me from speaking with her, you will suffer the consequences," said Remus. "For your sake, I suggest you tell her I'm here."

Remus looked over at Stephen and winked. It felt good to order around one of Grieves's snooty aides.

"What gift?" Stephen asked quietly. "We didn't bring a gift. I packed your backpack, remember?"

"Shh. I did bring a gift. I didn't tell you about it, but you'll find out soon enough."

Roger shook his head but got up anyway and went to speak with the president. Moments later, he came back red faced and apologetic.

"I apologize. I didn't realize who you were, sir. Please, follow me at once."

"Yeah, that's more like it." Remus pointed at Stephen. "He comes, too."

As Remus and Stephen entered the president's office, she stood up to greet them. Remus was shocked at this, as she'd never shown any deference or respect to him in their previous meetings. He'd have to make the most of the situation.

"Welcome back, Remus. It's good to see you," said the president.

"It's very good to be here, believe me. I've been through a lot the last few weeks, and that's why I'm here to report to you."

Indicating Stephen, he continued. "But before I give you any information, first let me tell you about this guy here. He is from the Sleeper group that escaped you and your security guards. Remember that incident, President Grieves?"

Grieves shifted, looking very uncomfortable, and Remus

had to suppress a smile. It was her turn to feel bad. His fantasy about this moment was coming true. He continued.

"Instead of waiting as you suggested, I went out immediately and continued to spy on the Sleepers. And just as I had predicted, they were leaving the next morning. Unfortunately I was caught by them and taken prisoner. The entire time I've been gone, they've been dragging me around by a rope tied around my neck. My neck! Treated me like a damned dog. Given my treatment by their group, I do not feel guilty about what I'm about to do, Madam President."

Glynis Grieves stiffened at Remus's use of the title. She hated to be called Madam. Remus knew that and had used the title on purpose.

"I offer you this young man as a prisoner. Do what you will with him to get information. I'd like to inform you that I know as much as he does. But in any case, he's all yours."

Poor Stephen looked over at Remus, seemingly confused, trying to determine whether Remus was a joking or not. *Idiot kid.*

"Excellent, Remus, excellent."

She pressed the button on her desk, and soon the room was filled with security guards.

"Take this man away and lock him in an empty office until I determine what to do with him," said Glynis.

"Why are you locking me in an office?" cried Stephen. "*I'm* the gift? What does this mean? Remus, I thought we were friends. I helped you even though you were our prisoner. Don't let them take me, please! Remember the great talks we had? How can you be this cold, Remus?"

Remus looked away, refusing to make eye contact with the kid. He refused to let any minuscule feeling of guilt affect what he assumed would be his new career in the Capital.

"Remus!" Stephen screamed as they pulled him away.

"Now, down to business, Glynis," said Remus, ignoring Stephen's fading cries. "May I call you Glynis?"

Her cheeks were getting red with anger, and she appeared to be weighing her options.

"No, Remus," she said coldly. "Despite this great gift and the information you are about to give me, I'm still the president. Everyone, including you, is to call me President Grieves."

The tone of her voice was enough to convince him. It was time to back off a bit. "Understood, President Grieves."

"Go on, Remus. Tell me what you know about the Sleepers."

Remus told her about their number, the names of all the Sleepers, their talents, and most importantly, their plan.

"They're planning to find an escape route through a door?" said Grieves. "There is no door!"

Liar. Guess that confirms that there is a door. I'll keep that information to myself.

He threw his hands up. "Hey, I'm just reporting what they were discussing. They were also trying to climb *over* the Wall, but so far they've not been successful. Their leader, Decker, described some sort of barrier that he can't cross, I heard him say there were spikes and barbed wire. But then, you'd know about that, wouldn't you?"

Glynis nodded.

"They're also searching for other Sleepers. I didn't hear anything more about that plan. When we escaped, they were heading toward the border between the North and East Sectors. Whether they know of another group or just are hoping there are others out there, is also unclear. But get this, they renamed themselves. The little band of Sleepers who dared to go against you, President Grieves, has now renamed themselves the Dreamers." He gave her a slight smirk.

Glynis Greaves laughed out loud. "They are quite proud

of themselves, aren't they?" She paused, drumming her fingers on the desk. "This information is very useful, Remus. As a reward, I would like you to work with my security guards. And if you do a good job, someday, and I mean someday soon, you may be assigned your own squadron. Until then, report to D Squadron on the second floor of this building."

"Thank you, President Grieves."

"Yes, well, move along. I have things to do."

"Yes, of course. Thank you again."

She waved her hand at him dismissively, but he barely noticed.

Remus walked out, proud of himself. The last time he left this building he'd scuttled out like a rat; this time he walked out with his chest out and his head high. He felt like a winner.

CHAPTER SIX

As Stephen was led away, he cursed himself in his head. All the choices he'd made in the last few days were wrong. He'd left a loving and safe group to follow Remus. In hindsight, he couldn't understand how he'd been seduced by Remus's talk of freedom. He'd thought they'd become friends, but instead he'd been duped into betraying his true friends.

Stephen slumped his shoulders, regretting his choices regarding the Dreamers. They'd never take him back after what he did. He'd never talk to Claudia again, or play with Marian's children. Never laugh around a campfire with a full belly and the security of friendship. Not caring what his guards thought of him, he wept. Remus's poisonous act had ruined the rest of his life, and he was ready to mourn that loss.

They arrived in front of a building which, according to his guards, the Sleepless would never see. The thought terrified him. What did they do to Sleepers in there? After passing through a set of heavy iron gates, they walked to the front door and rang a bell. The door opened, and then the guards took off Stephen's restraints, shoved him through, and slammed it behind him.

Stephen looked around. A tall, bulky man with horn-rimmed glasses entered the room and stopped a few feet away.

"You the new one?"

Stephen nodded while wiping the tears from his eyes.

"Can't you talk? I need you to confirm your name."

"I'm Stephen. Who are you?"

The tall man looked thoughtful, then answered. "Boss. Just Boss."

Boss led Stephen to his cell. Cement walls, no window, and a cement slab to sleep on. His toilet was lidless and made of steel. He was relieved to see toilet paper and yet guilty that something so basic would make him happy.

"Lights out at 9 p.m. Follow me to the mess hall. Just dump your bag on the floor."

The building was huge. They walked for ten minutes before they arrived in the mess hall. It was dinnertime, so Boss pointed to the food line. It was like a cafeteria. Metal trays and steam tables with that day's choice of food. It surprised Stephen to see food he hadn't eaten in a decade.

"Next!" said the cafeteria worker.

Stephen stepped up reluctantly, not sure what to do. "This is my first day, sir, what can I order?"

The cafeteria worker looked at Stephen and chuckled.

"This ain't no fancy restaurant, buddy. Tell me what meat, vegetable, and starch you want. That's it. Got it?"

Stephen nodded. "Meatballs, mashed potatoes, and broccoli, please."

After a surprisingly good meal, Boss gave Stephen a tour of the rest of the building. All except the workroom. He told him he would see that tomorrow.

"Breakfast is at 7 a.m. I'll be back at your room at 8 a.m.," said Boss, and with that, he walked away, leaving Stephen wholly confused. What kind of prison was this?

He was too scared to wander around on his own, so with nothing to do, he settled down on the slab and used his backpack as a pillow. He laid there thinking all afternoon and into the evening, struggling with his emotions and wondering what would happen the next day.

That night, Stephen dreamed about the Dreamers.

The next morning, Boss showed Stephen to the workroom. There were hundreds of others sitting at tables, working diligently. Why was he here? Was everyone else guilty of breaking the law? Stephen was still trying to figure out what was going on, but for now he was resigned to being there.

"Am I in prison?" he asked Boss.

"Let's just say you are a permanent guest. Now go to the office in the far corner and meet your supervisor. You won't see me again unless you make trouble."

Stephen was even more confused. A supervisor? As he approached the office, he looked at what the others were assembling. He did a double take. Everyone was making phones. Smartphones. The kind he used to own BIB. He spotted a vaguely familiar logo he hadn't seen in a very long time. They were Pippin Corp phones.

What the hell?

"Are you Stephen?" asked the supervisor.

Stephen looked at the nametag he was required to wear and wondered why the man bothered asking. He almost gave a biting remark but then decided it probably wasn't a good idea to mouth off on his first day. Who knew what they could do to him.

"Yes, I'm Stephen. I arrived yesterday."

"I know when you arrived. Just verifying who you are. Follow me to one of the tables. And no talking!"

The man didn't bother to tell Stephen his own name, leading him to the end of one of the long tables. He pointed to a chair. Stephen sat down and looked up at the supervisor, wondering what to do next.

"Okay, this work is very simple. So simple even a child could do it. In fact, back in the twentieth century, children *did* do this job." He pointed. "Take the tablet there, read the instructions. I'll give you two hours. After that I'd better see you working."

The supervisor walked away, leaving Stephen to his task. He picked up the tablet and began to swipe through it, reading the instructions to try to understand his new situation. Most of the instructions consisted of blueprints of the Pip15 phone. He assumed that was what he and all the others were assembling. It looked simple enough; a lot of the intricate work was done elsewhere. Stephen wondered if it was in another building just like this one, where others assembled the insides of the phones. In this building, all he needed to do was put the parts together. It was a lot like building a model. Then he had to polish it and put cling film on both sides so it wouldn't get scratched. He wasn't sure who put everything in the box, but that wasn't his problem for now.

Stephen looked around for a friendly face. No one was smiling, and everyone focused on their work, their faces blank. They seemed to have no emotions at all. He decided to try to strike up a conversation with the woman next to him, ignoring the supervisor's warning about talking.

"Hi there, my name is Stephen. What's yours?"

The dark-haired woman ignored his greeting and kept working.

"Hey, I'm just trying to be friendly. Don't you want to talk to me? It's awfully boring if all we do is put together these damn phones."

The woman turned her head slightly and looked him up and down. Then she turned back to her task. "My name is Monica," she whispered. "And we shouldn't be talking."

Encouraged by her speaking to him, Stephen replied in a whisper. "Nice to meet you, Monica. So how long have you been doing this?"

"I've been here for two years. Although I must tell you, it feels like twenty."

"What are you in for?"

Stephen thought he was being funny, but the look on Monica's face told him it was anything but.

"Are you kidding me? Did you just really ask me that? Either you're an idiot or you truly don't know why any of us are in here. Either way, keep this up and you'll have problems until someone sets you straight."

"Well, then, Monica, I'd appreciate it if you'd set me straight. What the heck is going on here? What is this place? I don't know what I did other than be a Sleeper. That's probably it. The guy that brought me into town is a rat. He outed me to President Grieves herself."

Before Monica could answer him, Stephen sensed someone standing behind him. He turned and saw the supervisor glaring at him.

"Follow me."

"Why?"

No reply came, and the man turned and walked away, so Stephen got up and followed. They headed out of the workroom, down the corridor, then turned left. A door automatically opened, and the supervisor pointed to the inside, indicating that Stephen was to go in there. It was a dark room, and he was expecting the lights to come on, but they didn't. The door slammed behind him, leaving Stephen in complete darkness. It was then he realized he was claustrophobic.

Stephen began to hyperventilate, but after a few minutes he managed to calm himself, and he began to explore the space. He walked with care until he bumped into one of the walls, ran his hands up and down the smooth surface, looking for anything. He was in a tiny 5' x 5' room, more like a closet, and he was stuck there until the supervisor decided he'd learned his lesson. Whatever that was.

The minutes rolled by, and it felt like an eternity. At one point he hyperventilated so much he almost fainted. When at last the door opened, Stephen fell to the floor, gasping for air. He felt so much gratitude for the supervisor that he had to stop himself from groveling at his feet. He'd heard of Stockholm Syndrome before, and he wasn't going to fall prey to that. Nevertheless, after his first punishment, he knew that rule breaking was not an option. Not if he wanted to keep his sanity.

The next morning at breakfast, Stephen sat down next to Monica. They were all allowed to speak during meal times and at the end of the day when the shift was over, so he intended to ask her more questions. She looked startled to see him but also glad. She had a nice smile, and Stephen hoped that it meant he had an ally and a friend in this dismal place.

"So, you survived the closet?" asked Monica.

"Holy shit, Monica, that was brutal. And all I did was *talk* to you. I'm glad you weren't punished as well. If they give that punishment for talking, I don't want to even think about what they do to anyone trying to escape from this place."

Monica looked stricken and scared at the mere mention

of escaping. "Don't even say that, Stephen. Some of the other workers are spies for the supervisor. They get extras like dessert and alcohol. Things that we don't have access to if they inform on us."

"So you're saying not to trust anyone? Then how do I know if I can trust you?"

"You don't. Do your work and stay quiet. It's the only way you'll survive this place, Stephen."

Every day it was the same. Wake up, eat breakfast, work on assembling phones. A fifteen-minute lunch break to eat an EnUR-G bar and drink water. Finish the day. Eat dinner. Go to bed. The work day was twelve hours. After his shift, Stephen could go to the recreation room and watch Nation-sponsored television. There wasn't much of a selection.

Channel 1: News

Channel 2: Sports

Channel 3: Government

Although curious about the sports station—he'd been a huge football fan BIB—Stephen didn't want to watch the Sector Series. Aidan had described the games in brutal, bloody detail. He'd tried to get the Dreamers to understand why he was so traumatized by his experience, and it worked. He wasn't the only one who felt that way. No one wanted to watch the games, either. Instead he watched the news, thinking he might see something about Remus, but he was disappointed. The anchor talked about the weather, how satisfactorily the crops were growing, and how well the Nation was doing. At least there were no reports of the missing Sleepers, which was good news.

Today, he chose to go straight to his room, lie down, and stare at the ceiling. The hour before lights out was the only time he had to himself, other than when he slept. He spent that precious time thinking about the life he'd left behind, regret his constant companion.

One day during work, he was daydreaming about his past life with the Sleepers, and he wasn't paying much attention to his task. Although it had only been a short amount of time, he'd memorized the steps to assemble the Pip5 phones. It was mindless, boring work.

An hour after his shift began, he dropped a phone. The sound of splintering glass and clattering plastic echoed throughout the large room. The other workers stopped what they were doing in anticipation of what would happen next.

The supervisor stalked over and pointed to the exit. Stephen knew he would be back in the closet. What he didn't know was for how long. When the closet door closed, he curled up into a ball and began to rock himself. If he wasn't broken yet, he soon would be. He tried to keep track of time by counting to sixty over and over. After the hundredth time, he gave up. Stephen wasn't tired, so sleep wasn't a viable escape. Instead his thoughts went back to the Dreamer camp and his friends. In his mind he apologized to each of them in the hope that they would somehow feel his thoughts and offer their forgiveness.

Moments after that, he heard a light tapping on the door. Not sure if he should answer, he remained silent and afraid. It could be Boss or the supervisor. Either way, he didn't want to know what would happen next.

CHAPTER SEVEN

Decker sat next to the remains of the night's fire, tapping his knee nervously as he went over in his mind how Remus could have escaped. Stephen had to have helped him, because he was also missing, and he couldn't imagine how Remus could have escaped with a prisoner. What confused Decker was why. Why would Stephen do it? Stephen didn't complain. He seemed to like the Dreamers and was never involved in any fights. The only time he'd disagreed with the group was when they voted on whether to accept Kate into their family. After that, he'd befriended her and didn't say anything more in protest.

He found Claudia and asked if she knew anything about Stephen's state of mind, but she told him that he'd seemed the same. Next, he went looking for Bridget to ask her about any insights about Stephen. He'd observed her easy way with everyone, and he thought that of anyone in the group, she'd be the one to notice a change.

"Do you mind if I come in, Bridget?" Decker called outside her tent.

He heard some rustling. "Sure, come on in. Just waking from a little cat nap."

Decker settled on the ground and waited until Bridget was fully awake.

"Look, Bridget, only a couple of people know this, so please keep it to yourself for now, but Remus escaped last night, and as far as I can tell, Stephen helped him. He's missing, too."

"And you want me to tell you if I know anything about it?"

Decker nodded. "Yes. I'm trying to understand why he'd do something like this."

Bridget nodded and closed her eyes for a couple of moments, concentrating. Decker sat there for a bit, feeling a bit awkward, not sure what she was doing.

"He feels guilty," she said after a minute.

"What? How would you know that, Bridget?"

She sighed. "Do you have a few minutes, Decker? I've been meaning to talk to you about something, but I could never find the right time. I think this is the perfect opportunity to tell you."

Decker raised his eyebrows in an unspoken question, then nodded. A nervous Bridget sat up straighter before she began to talk.

"I haven't spoken to anyone about this since the last group of Sleepers I lived with. In fact, not even Kate knows this about me yet. But don't worry, I'll tell her today. I have what I can only call a gift. I know things. My body tingles before the phone rings. I can feel a person approaching my door, and just before the person knocks, I open it. Am I psychic? Who knows? I was never one that believed in the supernatural, but I'm proof that there are things that cannot be understood." She smiled. "That's almost word for word the explanation I gave to Desmond."

Decker's head jerked up at the name.

"Funny, that's the name of my grandfather."

"I know," said Bridget in a low voice.

"Haven't seen him since BIB. I miss him." Then he realized what she'd said. "Wait, what do you mean you *know*? How could you know my grandfather's name? I never speak about him."

"Decker, the last group of Sleepers I lived with before finding you was near the Wall in the West Sector. Your grandfather is their leader. Interesting, isn't it, that both of you are leaders?"

He stood up, his face turning red. "Why didn't you tell me this sooner? We could have been heading west instead of east! How could you be so thoughtless!"

Bridget was stunned but didn't seem offended and recovered quickly. His mind reeled at the thought of his grandfather out there, and he couldn't contain his emotions.

"I'm sorry, Bridget," he said. "I shouldn't have said that. It's just this news is so unexpected."

"I had to be sure before I told you. And as I said, there never seemed to be the right time to say anything. When you and the others accepted me into your group, I needed to find out what kind of person you were. The reason I could survive and move amongst the different Sleeper groups is my ability to judge a person's character. If not for that skill, I'd be a prisoner in the Nation."

Decker fiddled with a corner of her sleeping bag, thinking. Finally, he nodded. "Of course. That makes sense. Tell me about him. How is he?"

"Your grandfather is an amazing man. He leads a group of Sleepers who have been together since the very beginning of this plague." She smiled and placed a hand on his knee. "Imagine that, Decker, they've been together for *ten* years. That speaks to his leadership skills. He spends every morning gardening." She smiled. "I see you're surprised at that."

Decker's brow was furrowed. "I am. He never had an interest in gardening BIB. I wonder why he changed? So what does he grow?"

The man Decker remembered was always busy. He never had time for something like gardening.

"He grows lettuce, carrots, zucchini," said Bridget. "Anything that supplements the diet of his Sleepers. Desmond says he finds gardening contemplative. But the two most important things for you to be aware of are these: he's healthy, and he misses you terribly."

"With your gift, were you able to tell him I was alive? What did he say about that?"

Her smile faltered slightly at his question. "My gift is limited. I can channel a person's feelings but not their location. That being said, I told him you were exhausted. My guess at the time was that you were one of the Sleepless. That news devastated him."

"If I was exhausted, it was probably after helping Kate during one of the cleanings."

"I know that now. But when I was telling Desmond about you, I didn't know any better. He was happy you were alive, but he was sad for you. We need to go back to his camp and get you two together. But first, I suggest we continue going east."

Decker frowned, not sure why Bridget would make that suggestion. "But why not go back to the west and reunite with my grandfather? He shouldn't have to suffer without knowing any longer. And for that matter, *I* shouldn't suffer any longer, either. I miss that old man and want to see him."

"Decker, the reason I've survived this long is because I don't let emotions get in my way. If I'd listened to my emotions, I'd still be with Desmond's group. But then I wouldn't have found Kate. Your heart says to go to your grandfather, but what does your mind say, Decker?"

Decker sat still, weighing the possibilities of what the group should do next. Not a selfish person, he tried to put the needs of the Dreamers first. But the chance to see his grandfather weighed heavily on him. At last, he decided.

"You're a wise woman, Bridget. We need to continue east to see if we can find another group of Sleepers. I'm guessing that if Desmond—it's so strange to call him by his first name —knew of a door, they would've told you. He wouldn't be complacent and not want to explore if he had information about a possible escape from the Nation. Knowing what I know about Grandpa, he'd want to go somewhere where he could actively look for a cure for the Sleepless. Especially since he thinks I'm one of them."

Bridget smiled. "You know your grandfather quite well. Desmond's curiosity wouldn't allow him to sit by and do nothing if he thought he could help his group. I knew you'd understand."

The urge to be selfish and change course wasn't entirely gone, but Decker knew the well-being of the Dreamers had to come first.

"And since you've been with them, we also know that his group is friendly, so we gain nothing other than my reunion if we went straight to his encampment." Decker nodded as it all started to make more sense as he talked about it. He shook his head. "I just wish there were some way to send word to him so he wouldn't continue to worry about me. But then it would be a waste of resources. We can't send any of our people, so he'll just have to wait as well." He looked up at her with a hopeful smile. "It will make our reunion that much sweeter when we finally meet up again."

Bridget patted him on a knee. "I'm going to go find Kate now and tell her about my gift. I hope she isn't angry I didn't explain this to her years ago. After that, feel free to tell the rest of the group about me. I can offer what I offered

Desmond's group, which is to take the name of one family member and use my gift to determine whether they're alive or deceased."

He looked at her, surprised. "You'd do that for us?"

She laughed. "Of course! Though I don't think I'm going to make more guesses about whether they're Sleepers are not, after the debacle of guessing wrong about you. How about we meet by the campfire in about an hour?"

Decker nodded. "Thank you, Bridget."

Decker gathered the Dreamers around the campfire, telling them it was time for a meeting. They brought their dinners with them and waited, curious, since Decker seemed to be excited about something. There was a nervous energy about him.

"I have some shocking news to share with you. Last night Remus and Stephen left us."

The group erupted in gasps and cries of shock. Decker held his hands up to quiet them. "I'm trying to give him the benefit of the doubt, but at this point I'm pretty sure Stephen helped Remus escape. What I'm not sure about is why. My best guess is that Remus somehow twisted Stephen's way of thinking and lured him away from us. That'll be the first thing I ask him, when, not if, we see him again."

Decker looked around, noting the faces full of anger and hurt. He was silently grateful that he had Bridget's gift to help temper their emotions.

"But something else came out of this. While asking Bridget what she thought about Stephen, she revealed something to me that I want her to tell all of you about."

Decker nodded to Bridget. She stood up in the center of

their circle and began to speak, giving the Dreamers a shortened version of what she'd told Decker.

Decker watched the faces of the Dreamers while Bridget spoke. Clearly they were intrigued. Thankfully, no one seemed afraid of her gift.

"The reason Decker and I wanted to let you know about this ability of mine," continued Bridget, "is that it can be used to help all of you. If you will give me the name and a description of a loved one you'd like me to try to contact, I'll do my best for you. But let me say this: I can't tell you where they are, only *how* they are."

Bridget paused to look at the Dreamers. They waited silently for her to go on.

"In other words, I can tell you if they are alive, and what they're feeling at the moment. I channel their emotions. Come to me privately one at the time, and I'll get started. Given the number of people in our group, this will take more than a few days."

They streamed in and out of her tent all day. Each one had a family member that Bridget tried channeling. It began the same way each time. The Dreamer gave her the name and description, then Bridget closed her eyes. A couple of them grabbed her hand while she concentrated. Then a familiar tingling throughout her body signaled she was about to receive an emotion.

After consulting with ten Dreamers, she had to turn the rest away until the next day. Trying to reach so many people in one day exhausted her. In the first day's session, she managed to get a sense for all ten. No dead family members. Bridget was relieved. Kate walked in with a cup of tea for her.

"Thank you, dear."

Kate nodded. Then she stood there awkwardly, watching Bridget sip the tea. Finally she said, "We need to talk, Bridget."

"What about?"

"I know you're tired but ... What is Stephen feeling right now?"

Bridget nodded. It was a fair request, and she could do one more. She closed her eyes, and after a few seconds felt a jolt instead of a tingling. She gasped.

"Oh! Oh no."

Kate reached for her. "What is it?"

"It's horrible!" Bridget put a hand to her head, clearly in distress. "I need to clear my head. He's ... he's frightened. But not just frightened, he's terrified. He also feels trapped."

"They must have captured him. I need to tell Decker right way. Can you tell me where he is? It would make everything so much easier."

Bridget shook her head. "If I had that power I would've found you ten years ago, my dear girl."

"I haven't talked to anyone about it, but I would guess there are more than a few of us who feel betrayed by his actions." Kate's shoulders slumped. "I have to admit, *I* feel a bit betrayed. I know he didn't want me to join the group, but once I did, I thought we'd become friends."

Bridget put her arm around Kate. "Stephen had a good heart. Don't let this change what you think of him too much."

Kate pursed her lips, her brow furrowing. "If he was tricked by Remus, then we underestimated our prisoner."

CHAPTER EIGHT

The next morning, as they were breaking down the campsite, Jeremy spotted a plume of smoke rising from deep within the forest. They'd been walking for weeks and had yet to find other Sleepers. He tempered his excitement with caution. Were they Sleepers or President Grieves's goons? He needed to ask Decker what to do. Aidan was standing nearby when he found Decker, so Jeremy motioned the pair over and had them follow him to a spot near the Wall.

"Did you notice it?" Jeremy asked.

Both nodded.

"What should we do, Decker?" Aidan asked.

"I need both of you to head over and find out who's living there. I hope it's other Sleepers, but you need to be careful. For all we know it could be an unstable group."

"What, like cannibals or something?"

Decker gave him a weird look, then laughed. "Aidan, I think your imagination is getting the best of you. Or was that a joke?"

"A dumb joke, sorry. It seems no one laughs much anymore. Sure, we can go, right, Jeremy?"

Jeremy was trying not to laugh at Aidan's joke, so he simply nodded.

"You should leave now before anybody notices you're gone. I don't want people worrying," said Decker. "Be safe."

The two of them nodded and set out in the direction of the smoke.

"What if this is a group of Sleepers?" asked Aidan. "Do you think they'll talk to us?"

"I hope so. We're not scary guys. You look like a nice, all-American dude, Aidan. And I look like a computer geek, glasses and all. Actually, since there isn't an internet café around here for miles, maybe I *will* scare them."

Aidan laughed at that. "I guess. But still, having a couple of strangers show up at their camp might freak them out. Remember, your group—I guess it's mine now, too—didn't trust me."

Jeremy nodded, and they continued on, occasionally pointing out things to each other. As they got closer, they moved silently, concentrating on not snapping sticks on the ground or startling any animals. Jeremy looked over at Aidan, impressed at his ability to move with such stealth. He didn't think a city boy would possess those skills. Jeremy made a note not to judge people based on where they came from. He also realized how much he liked Aidan. He was the kid brother he never had.

After half an hour, Jeremy motioned for them to stop. They squatted down near a tree and began forming a plan.

"How far out do you think we are?" asked Jeremy.

"It's farther than it looks," said Aidan, "probably a couple of miles. I'm guessing this group lives on the border between North and East Sectors. Let's slow down in case they have any lookouts in the woods. If we move too fast, we'll look threatening."

Jeremy nodded. Then they heard someone giggling to their left. Jeremy pointed to the bushes and put his finger to his lips to shush Aidan. As soon as their eyes met, he realized how stupid it was to pretend they hadn't been seen.

"Yes, we're two guys walking along, laughing, not looking for any trouble," Jeremy said with a sigh. "Who's there?"

More giggling.

"Nope, we wouldn't hurt a fly. Think it's a fly?" Aidan asked Jeremy as they both stood.

"Never knew a fly to giggle," said Jeremy. They saw a bush wiggling nearby.

Aidan walked over and found a girl hanging back in the bushes. She had trouble making eye contact with them. Her long blonde hair hid her face. Her petite frame seemed even smaller as she slouched in the shadows.

"Hey, I'm Aidan, what's your name?"

The giggling stopped, and the smile dropped from her face. Aidan's outstretched hand hung in the air unanswered. He let it drop and moved his eyes from her face to her feet.

"I'm Kirsten," she said in a quiet voice.

Jeremy approached Kirsten. "So, uh, what's so funny?"

No answer.

"It's okay, we're not mad, just curious," said Aidan.

She shrugged. "You two looked goofy. I could tell you were trying to look tough, but instead you look like a couple of nice nerdy guys."

Jeremy sighed. "See?" he said, looking at Aidan. "I knew it. I suppose we should let you know that we're with a group of Sleepers. Hope that makes you feel better about us. Now, do you feel safe enough to take us to your leader, Kirsten?"

Kirsten giggled again, then began to walk back to her camp. Aidan and Jeremy followed her. After thirty minutes, they were on the outskirts of the camp. Kirsten motioned for them to stop. "Wait here. And *don't* move."

She continued on by herself. When she returned, she was with a slight woman in her sixties with short gray hair, dressed in army fatigues. She stepped forward, demanding Aidan and Jeremy identify themselves. Her eyes were shaded by a Yankees baseball cap. Her demeanor made her seem like the leader.

"We're just here to talk, ma'am," said Aidan.

The woman burst out laughing. "I haven't been called ma'am in years. Definitely not since AIB. What are you, about sixteen or seventeen?"

"Sixteen, ma'am. Would you like me to call you something else?" asked Aidan.

"You're not getting my name until I know more about both of you. First, your names."

"I'm Aidan, and this is my friend Jeremy. He's a Sleeper."

"And?"

"And what, ma'am?"

"And where's your camp?" she said, putting her hands on her hips. Her voice was tinged with impatience. "Who's your leader? Why are you here?"

Aidan was about to answer again, but Jeremy took over.

"What's with the hostility? We've been polite; we didn't harm Kirsten. Why are you treating us like criminals?"

The woman looked Jeremy up and down before replying in a sharp tone. "You're a rather feisty young man, aren't you? I—*we*—can't afford to trust anyone. You could be practiced liars, or paid informants of President Grieves. So answer my questions, and then I can decide whether to welcome you or send you away."

"We are from a group that used to live due west of your camp," said Jeremy. "That is, until a few weeks ago. Since then we've been on the move looking for other Sleepers."

"Why?"

"Because we wanted to know if there were any, and if so, see if they wanted to join forces. Share resources and information, that kind of thing."

"Go on," said Yankee Hat.

"Our leader is a guy named Decker." Jeremy put his hands on his hips. "I think we've told you quite enough about us. Can we get your name now?"

As Jeremy spoke with the older woman, he noticed Aidan was whispering to Kirsten. *Oh great, he's got a crush. Not the time, Aidan.*

"My name is Arlene."

"Nice to meet you, Arlene ..."

"Just Arlene. We stopped using last names years ago. You're the first visitors in over a year. Sorry for the hostility. Kirsten told me you were a couple of nice guys, but I had to check that out myself."

"So ... do we pass the test, then?" asked Aidan.

Arlene nodded. "For now. I'm a pretty good judge of character." She motioned with her head. "Follow us, and I'll introduce you to the rest of our community."

Jeremy relaxed a bit. Now that Arlene had introduced herself, it meant she trusted them, at least enough to reveal her name. They followed her to the camp and were surprised by how small it was. There were only eight tents as far as he could see, and no more than a couple of occupants per tent. Arlene appeared to be the oldest of the group, and Kirsten was the youngest. Although the group was small, they didn't seem to want for anything. The tents were in good condition, there was a robust fire with what looked to be some sort of bird roasting, and a bunch of wild greens sitting next to a pile of hand-woven baskets. No one looked grubby. All seemed clean and healthy.

"So how long have you all been living in this camp, Arlene?" Aidan asked.

"I've been here since the very beginning, and about half of this group have been here with me. The rest are wanderers like you, who happened upon our camp and decided to stay with us. Only one person has ever left our group after finding us. A woman who was here about five years ago."

It dawned on Jeremy that he knew who Arlene was referring to.

"Was it Bridget?" he asked.

Arlene looked surprised. "Yes, how did you know?"

"Because she's part of our group now. She told us that she wandered through all the sectors and met several groups, so it was an educated guess. I bet she'd love to see you again," said Jeremy. "You want to come to our camp and reunite with her and meet some of our people? Our group is much larger than yours, but we're friendly and willing to share information and any supplies you might need."

Arlene pursed her lips a bit, thinking things over. After a bit, she said, "Sit tight."

Jeremy watched Arlene call her group together in a huddle on the far side of the camp and talk for a while. He supposed they were trying to decide if they wanted to go with them to meet his group and were trying to determine if he and Aidan were telling the truth. After five minutes or so, Arlene returned to their side.

"I'll come with you, and Kirsten insists on coming along, too. But before we go, let me show you some of our hospitality."

Kirsten and a couple of the other Sleepers brought over some of the roast bird and a simple salad. They also brought over some homemade wine.

"Well, I'm not twenty-one yet, but I suppose it doesn't matter anymore, right?" said Aidan.

Jeremy laughed. "When I was your age, I would've been excited if someone offered me wine. Go for it!"

After a delicious dinner and interesting conversation, the four of them got ready to depart. Before they left, Jeremy decided it was a good time to tell Arlene about their new group name.

"Hey, Arlene? You got a minute?"

Arlene finished up giving some instructions to one of the Sleepers, then turned to him. "What is it?"

"I wanted to tell you a bit about Decker before we leave, just so you know what to expect. He's only been with our group for a few years. Longer than me, but he hasn't been there from the beginning. When he arrived, he was a natural leader, and the group accepted him, and when I joined the group, I knew right away he was the best person to lead us."

Arlene said nothing, which Jeremy was still getting used to.

"Don't forget that he's idealistic, kind, and determined," Aidan said, seemingly to break the silence.

"Anyway, few days ago, he had an idea which we all liked. We decided to call ourselves the Dreamers. It's an important new distinction for us. Since we're, you know, dreaming of a new future."

Arlene cracked a rare smile. "Dreamers, huh? I think I like that idea. It speaks of hope."

Jeremy smiled. He'd hoped she'd understand.

Arlene and some of her group followed Jeremy to the Dreamers' camp. During the one-hour walk, the two groups chatted and got to know each other better. Jeremy was excited for the rest of their friends to meet and wondered if they'd get along as well as this small group did. There was no reason for them not to like one another, unless Arlene wasn't telling him the truth about her Sleepers.

"Aidan, do you mind if I ask you a question?"

"No, not at all, Arlene. What do you want to know?"

"Where is your family?"

Aidan looked at the ground. "They're uh ... they live in North City."

"I see. And yet you're out here on your own?"

"Yeah, it's ... sort of a long story."

Arlene nodded, then after a while, she asked, "Do you miss them?"

"Of course I miss them. I chose to leave North City for a couple of reasons, but I would say the most important was I couldn't live in that society any longer. Do you know what the Sector Series is?"

"Yes, unfortunately I do. I've never witnessed them, and I hope never to do so. I've had the event described to me, and I still don't understand the point of it."

"Well, I won the series this year."

Arlene stopped in her tracks and gripped his shoulder tightly. "Aidan, I'm so sorry."

Aidan nodded, and he was surprised to realize that he felt okay talking about it with Arlene, even though they'd just met. "Anyway, killing other kids ... it woke me up. It made me realize that none of it made sense. I was too ashamed to go back to my family and didn't know what to do next. Then one day I saw Decker cleaning up after my event. He just seemed different to me. I was curious about him, and something about him made me suspect he might be one of the Sleepers."

Arlene looked a bit surprised by that. "What about Decker made you think he was a Sleeper?"

Aidan shrugged. "Just a hunch. But the main thing that drew me to him was the fact that he was doing the cleaning for someone else. Never heard of someone doing that. It's a hideous task, and he seemed to be, well, I wouldn't say happy, but he seemed to be okay with it. That made me suspicious. And after he left, and I decided I needed to leave the city, I decided to look for them. And the rest, as they say, is history."

Jeremy joined their conversation. "He's a good kid, isn't he?" he asked, smiling at Arlene.

Arlene smiled back at him. "Yes, he is."

"Glad you two are getting along."

The rest of the journey felt easier to them all.

CHAPTER NINE

"Arlene, has any of your group attempted to climb the Wall?" Decker asked.

That morning, most of Arlene's Sleepers had returned with her to meet the Dreamers. They huddled around her, watching the Dreamers warily. The initial meeting the day before had gone well, and Arlene decided to bring her whole group over today.

"We've made some attempts, but nothing really happened. Some of our younger members try occasionally but none of us have ever had any real experience with climbing in our lives BIB, and I didn't want anyone injuring themselves. What about you?"

"I did try to climb fairly high up the other day but discovered my path was blocked by spikes."

"Spikes?"

"Yes, and it was clear that they were intentionally put there to prevent escape. Isn't that odd? Why would President Grieves care about any of us escaping if there truly is nothing on the other side of the Wall? If we want to kill ourselves, why should she care?"

Arlene narrowed her eyes. "That's an interesting question."

"I've been mulling this over. I think it's important that we figure out how to get to the top and see what really is over there."

Both groups stared at him with looks of surprise and some anxiety. As far as any of them knew, the Nation and the surrounding woods was all that was left of the United States. Hearing Decker's thoughts and trying to picture what was beyond the huge garbage wall was unsettling to say the least.

Finally, Arlene broke the silence. "What are you thinking, Decker?"

"I don't know, but I do know that Grieves is the last person we should be listening to."

Arlene chuckled. "I've never really been the type to just buy into her bullshit. I agree, we need to figure out a way to get over the Wall. Our group has a supply of some ropes that we've gathered—or rather, stolen—from East City. We can look through the garbage wall for anything that resembles a pickax or some type of climbing implement."

Decker dipped his head in agreement. He looked over at the Wall and wondered again what could be beyond.

"Also, I remember seeing some ladders along the Wall," Arlene continued. "Using a combination of any of those might give us the advantage we need. So, although I'm not really volunteering myself, once we set up something that looks stable, I'll give it a go. This old bird isn't finished yet."

Most of the group smiled at that statement. He noticed her Sleepers were starting to relax around them. Decker felt at ease, warmed by her enthusiasm.

"Okay," he said, "let's start taking inventory and gather whatever useful objects that we have together in one spot. Jeremy here is the most technically inclined of our group. Do you have some people like that in yours, Arlene?"

She simply nodded.

Decker continued. "I think it would be interesting for them to draw up some plans, and we can go from there. Our supply of paper is almost nonexistent, and Bridget's still working on making us some, but for now they could find a clear area and sketch some things out in the dirt. What do you think of that?"

"Hell yeah!" said Jeremy. "I'll do that. I love creating and trying to solve problems. Remember when we got together and built the imitator?"

"What's the imitator?" asked Arlene.

Jeremy sat up a little straighter, obviously eager to tell the story. "Well, I designed a little silver box the size of a deck of cards. It's a machine that loads the details of the task someone needs to do onto their drive so they get credit. That's how Decker was able to do Kate's cleanups in the stadium after a Sector Series."

Arlene seemed impressed. None of her group was *that* technically inclined. They'd all used computers and smartphones, but BIB, no one in Arlene's group had any technical training. No engineers or computer scientists among them.

"Wait, what if you don't have a port?" Arlene said. "How would that work? There are some of us who never lived in any of the cities and didn't have ports put in our heads. Thank God I never had one of those drilled into my skull."

"I thought of that, too. I designed a hat with a strap, which holds the imitator in place. There are silver dots inside. They read what your eyes see by accessing your brain and relaying the information to the flash drive. Pretty cool, right?"

"Pretty damn cool, Jeremy," said Arlene.

It was time to start planning, so Decker divided the group into those who would be trying to figure out a way over the Wall and others who were willing to build whatever was needed.

"Jeremy, I want you to select someone who you think would be good at designing. And if it's only you, then, thanks, brother." Decker slapped him on the back playfully. "You've got a lot of work to do." Decker laughed.

"I used to build a lot of Legos and tinker toys," said Aidan. "That might be useful since I was pretty creative with those things. I built amazing structures when I was a kid."

"Hey, I'll take all the help I can get. Let's head over to the patch of dirt I cleared and start drawing up plans."

Jeremy and Aidan went off to plan while the rest of the group started looking through the garbage wall for anything that might prove useful.

"Look, Mommy, look! I found a metal bar. Would it be helpful?" asked Oliver.

Marian smiled at her child and nodded.

"Ah! There are a couple of ladders over here," said Arlene, "and I think I see a hatchet under that broken door. Actually, I'll look for another door; that might help. It seems like it would be useful."

For the next hour, everyone enthusiastically built a pile of the garbage they found. Decker stopped to stretch and smiled, happy to see his group join together with another for a common cause. He had a good feeling about this and knew that they would make it to the top of the Wall. Decker looked around for Arlene and saw her talking to Claudia. He was pleased to see her jumping right in. The girl Aidan and Jeremy had first met, Kirsten, was doing the same, although he also noticed that every few minutes she looked over at Aidan. He chuckled. There was a romance blooming between those two.

Kate walked up and called out to the group. "Anyone hungry? I've got a big batch of stew going and I need all of you to come help me eat it."

All work stopped as everyone rushed back toward the

camp and the smell of a delicious rabbit stew. Kate had finally figured out how to catch a rabbit by using a bow and arrow she found in the Wall. She'd been practicing by shooting arrows into targets carved into the trees.

With a mouthful of food, Jeremy excitedly explained what he and Aidan had come up with. "So we've decided to use the concept of cantilevers. Before anyone asks, essentially we will be building a little platform so that when you get to the location of the iron spikes, you step out onto this platform. Then you lie on a board on top of the spikes, throw a grappling hook—we can make one of those from the metal that you all found—and then climb over the barrier."

"Yeah, and we already tested a small version of it at the bottom of the Wall, so we're pretty excited," said Aidan. "I think this is going to do it. The question is, who's gonna go first?"

All eyes went to Decker. He was going to volunteer anyway, but it felt great to know that they felt he was the best candidate.

"Let's finish our lunch first," he said, "then we'll go over and see the model that Aidan and Jeremy built. And if it looks like it can work, then we'll spend the next couple hours building what they've designed."

"Before we go any further," said Kate, "Jeremy, can you explain in a little more detail what a cantilever is, please? I'm not an engineer, and I think I've heard of the term but I have no idea what it is, even though you told us a little already. I need layman's terms."

"Okay, no problem. This will be a very basic explanation, just enough so you understand how it works."

There was a lot of head nodding. Jeremy took it as a sign to go on.

"When you cantilever something, it's only attached on one end. Before you freak out, think of something like a balcony. A lot of small balconies and decks are cantilevered. Of course, if it's a huge deck, there's posts underneath supporting the structure. Does that make sense to everyone?"

"It does to me," said Decker.

Jeremy turned to the rest to see if anyone was looking confused. Satisfied that everyone was following, he continued.

"Aidan, why don't you explain the next part? Our plan for getting up the Wall."

Aidan stepped into the middle of the circle of Dreamers. "We'll need to find a sturdy pole, probably one made of metal, like an old pipe. Decker will then climb up to the obstruction farther up the Wall. Once he finds a hole somewhere in the vicinity of the iron spikes, he can push the pole in. Once the pole is shoved in, he should be able to step on it, and then the person behind him will hand him up a board of some sort." Aidan made motions like how he expected Decker to move once up there. "We have to decide who's going to follow them up the Wall. Anyway, by putting this plank over the obstruction, he should be able to then climb over it and get to the top. If Decker finds that it's fairly easy, then more of us can go up and see what's up there."

"Sounds like as good a plan as any," said Decker. "Any volunteers to climb the Wall behind me?"

Decker was hoping Kate would volunteer but didn't want her to feel obligated.

Instead, Bridget stepped forward. "Me, Decker. I used to climb mountains, and I've been hiking for the last ten years. My arms are strong, and I'm as surefooted as a mountain goat. And some say as stubborn, too!"

Decker smiled. "You're the perfect backup for me, Bridget. Thanks for volunteering. How are your shoes? Are they flexible enough to grip the Wall?"

"They'll work. Let's get going," said Bridget. "We've got some pipes to find."

Everyone gathered at the foot of the Wall to watch. Decker strapped a metal pipe to his back and climbed. Once he reached the curved iron spikes, he untied the pipe and looked up. The spikes looked to be about five feet high. Finding a hole in the Wall near his waist, Decker wedged the pipe between two rusted appliances. He tested the support, and it didn't move much. Jeremy had insisted he test the pipe to be sure it wouldn't flip out.

"Take a breath. You've got this!" someone below yelled.

Right. I got this. With that thought, he hoisted his body onto the pipe. He checked out the top of the curved spikes and found a spot to climb up. The barbed wire wound around most of the spikes wasn't present at this spot.

He looked over his shoulder. "Never mind the board, Bridget. Come up and we'll go to the top together."

Decker watched Bridget scramble up the Wall. He chuckled. "You really are as nimble as a mountain goat."

"Glad you find that funny," she said as she hoisted herself up. "Okay, what's the plan from here? I'm not tall enough to climb over the spikes."

"Ah, but I can be your ladder. Here ... step onto my hands and I'll lift you high enough to get over. Be careful of the barbed wire. That opening is only two feet wide."

Bridget stepped on his hands and then gave a little whoop as he lifted her up. He scrambled up after her, thankful for his height and strength. He could hear the Dreamers cheering below.

"Well, that worked nicely," said Bridget. "What do you say, Decker? Shall we go to the top and solve the mystery of what is really on the other side?" She smiled.

Decker smiled back, hoping for good news, but he prepared himself for the worst. Ten years of living in the Nation did that to a person, even an optimist like Decker. "Yes. Are you ready for what might be out there?"

"I'm as ready as anyone can be. Let's do this."

Unplanned, they joined hands as they moved to the top. At the apex of the Wall, they had a clear view of the world outside.

Decker found himself at a complete loss for words. Down below was an expanse of trees, but past it was the last thing Decker expected. It was a city. And not just a city, but a *working* city. There were intact buildings. Freeways full of cars moved to unknown destinations. And he could even see in the distance a huge lake. With *sailboats.*

"This ... this doesn't make any sense." He looked to Bridget, who looked as confused as he felt.

"Do you recognize this place?"

"Yes, this is Chicago. But I keep thinking my eyes are playing tricks on me. I can't believe we've been living this close to the city. *My* city. I grew up there."

Bridget shook her head sadly. "This is crazy. I was expecting ruin. Maybe just forest, but not this."

"How are we going to tell the others the world still exists? That they've wasted the last ten years believing a lie?"

"I don't know, Decker." She paused, then a hint of a grin appeared on her face. "But do you know what I do know, Decker?"

"What?"

"I'd kill for a Chicago Dog right about now."

Decker blinked at her for a few seconds, then burst into laughter. He felt better with the tension broken, and the shock finally began to wear off.

"I think we can get everyone over the Wall, don't you, Decker? We don't need a door if we can all come this way."

"Sure, maybe if we—" He stopped, his blood going cold. As he spoke, he looked down at the other side of the Wall. His shoulders slumped, and he felt the excitement of a few minutes ago draining away. Peppered down the side of the Wall on the city side were large black devices with red lights on them—mines. The Wall wasn't just there to keep them from seeing the outside world; it was there to keep them from escaping.

They'd have to find the door after all.

"What we're about to tell you may be hard to hear."

The Dreamers murmured, then sat in a circle around Decker.

"When we climbed to the top of the Wall, we discovered two important things." He paused, then continued. "The other side of the Wall is booby trapped, so we'll have to continue on our journey to find a door. If it exists. The other thing"—he nodded at Bridget— "we're still trying to wrap our heads around. There is life on the other side of the Wall. *Normal* life. Like how things were BIB. Let that sink in. We've been lied to."

Everyone began to talk at once, wanting to know more about what they'd seen. Decker knew they'd be up all night talking about it.

CHAPTER TEN

When Stephen had run off with Remus a few days ago, it had shocked the Dreamers to their core. Since that day, it seemed to Decker that no one mentioned his name, as though they were attempting to forget him. No one wanted to admit their feelings of betrayal. But Decker didn't forget. Stephen was in his thoughts every day, and he wondered what he as a leader could've done to keep Stephen faithful to the group.

Decker refused to let it go and consider Stephen a lost cause. It was time to go find their friend and try to convince him to return to the fold.

"Hey, everyone, thanks for coming to this little meeting. This concerns my group of Dreamers, but Arlene, if you guys want to sit in and help us make a decision or just listen to what we're going through, that's fine with me."

His group sat down, and some of Arlene's group joined as well. Decker noticed Arlene hung back a bit. She was close enough to listen but not close enough to participate. She probably didn't want to overshadow his leadership, and was he thankful for that courtesy.

"Stephen's been gone a few days now, and before anyone argues with me"—he put up a hand—"I still consider him part of our group. Up until this incident, he'd never done anything to make us doubt him. He's always been a kind, considerate member of our family. I want to find him to see if I can convince him to rejoin us."

Several people started talking at once. Most of them were still reeling from the revelation of the Wall and the outside, and they wanted to focus on that.

"Okay, okay! Stop!" Decker sighed. "I knew this might cause some problems. Look, we can have a discussion, but my mind is made up. If we're going to work to get out of the Nation, I think Stephen still deserves to be with us. We have to find him and tell him what we've discovered. Plus, he might be in danger. Claudia, what do you have to say about this?"

"Decker, I just want to say that I support you. I was shocked when Stephen left." She looked around at the group. "Everyone was. But I agree that there's a chance he could still be saved. That Remus fellow was a sneaky rat, and I could see him turning Stephen's head. And I admit, if we made it out of here and left him behind, I don't know if I could live with it."

"Anyone else?" asked Decker.

No one said anything. They must've agreed with Claudia. Either that or they were unwilling to voice what they really thought of Stephen.

"Well, I've thought of a plan, and there's only one member of this group that can help me do it." He turned to Kate. "Are you willing to join me? You know it could be dangerous, but I don't think I can do this without you."

Kate stood up to face the group. "I agree with Decker's

assessment of Stephen, and yes, of course I'll go." She smiled. "All of you have given me so much. Protected me, introduced me to a new life, freed me from the awful tasks I used to do for sleep. There's no way I could say no. You'd do the same for me."

Bridget waved her hand to get Decker's attention.

"Hold on there, Decker. I'm not letting Kate out of my sight again. I'm going with you two, and there's nothing you can say that will stop me. Got it?"

Decker and Kate looked at each other, then smiled, an unspoken agreement between them.

"Well, then, I guess it's been decided," said Decker. "While we're gone, I'm putting Claudia and Jeremy in charge of the group. Any objections?"

"But what about the Wall? What about the door?" someone asked.

Decker sighed. "The Wall has been there for ten years. Yesterday we had no idea what was beyond it. Delaying getting out there can wait a few more days if it means Stephen can come, too, right?"

The group murmured in agreement.

He turned to Claudia and Jeremy. "What do you say?"

Jeremy took Claudia's hand, surprising her. "Yeah, we got this. Right, Claudia?"

Claudia squeezed Jeremy's hand. "Absolutely!"

The next morning, the trio prepared for their rescue mission. Decker filled his backpack with food, his sketch book, and the only weapon he ever carried: a hunting knife. He'd never had to use it on a human and hoped that wouldn't be changing anytime soon. Right before leaving his tent he remembered to grab some extra Somnum for Kate.

"Here, catch." Decker tossed the pills to Kate.

"Oh, good, I forgot about those. To be honest, I didn't know what to bring other than clothes. My part of the plan revolves around me being persuasive and looking clean enough to work in the Capital." Kate turned to her grandmother. "What did you pack?"

"Some snacks, clothes, and bandages. Not being a pessimist, but I want to be prepared in case one of us gets injured."

Decker nodded. "Nothing like that should happen, but it's good you're prepared. Thank you."

The plan was to return to North City, although East City was closer at this point. Kate had to be in a familiar city for her to be able to accomplish her part of the plan.

The long hike was surprisingly pleasant, each of them taking turns telling stories of their life BIB.

"Bridget, would you tell me more about my grandfather?" asked Decker. "We haven't had a chance to talk about him more, and I'm really curious how he's doing."

"Oh, there's so much I want to tell you about him. Desmond is a natural leader, just like you, Decker. His group respects him, they listen to him, and if it weren't for him I think they would've dispersed. He listens to his Sleepers. Truly listens," said Bridget. "And yet, because his decisions are so well thought out, there doesn't seem to be a reason to discuss them at times. I mentioned to you before that he likes to garden. Apparently his life as an ER doc was pretty stressful, so it's a relaxing hobby for him."

Decker shook his head with a smile. "That's so weird to me. I mean, growing up, he never even had house plants! I wonder what drew him to farming? That's something I've gotta ask when we eventually meet up with them. What else? Does he have a partner? Are there any other children in his life? I want to know as much as possible about him, Bridget."

Decker looked over and saw Bridget blushing. *Wonder what that's about?*

"When I met him, he didn't have a partner, so the last I knew, he was on his own. Don't know if there's any other children out there; that was never part of our conversations." She smiled.

"What is it?"

Bridget's cheeks became an even darker shade of pink. "I'm embarrassed to say this to you, but I was actually pretty attracted to your grandfather."

"Oh," said Decker, a weird look crossing his face.

Kate laughed. "Smooth, Decker."

"Oh, but nothing came of it because I had to keep moving," said Bridget. "I was looking for Kate. She has been and always will be my priority. As for his health, he looks great. He doesn't have any health problems." Bridget smiled again, remembering Desmond.

"Does he seem happy?"

"Except for missing you, he seems pretty happy. I'm still really upset that I gave him the wrong information about you and said you were Sleepless. I'm sure I added another layer of worry that he just doesn't need."

Decker put his arm around her.

"You were trying to help the group," said Kate. "Don't beat yourself up over it. You did a good thing for those Sleepers; you gave them some sense of closure. Yes, some of them found out their loved ones were dead, but remember, the majority of them found out that they still have someone out there that's alive. Think of the joy you brought them."

Decker knew Bridget needed reassuring. She'd kept the burden of her gift to herself for too long.

"She's right, Bridget. I'm anxious to go west and meet up with my grandfather, but the mere thought that he is out there and alive gives me more joy than you can imagine. First, we'll get Stephen, and then we can head west to find Desmond and his group." His face hardened with determination. "And then we're going to get out of here."

They continued walking. Birds chirped in the forest, and for a while the only sound they made were the light footsteps in the dirt.

"Hey, Bridget," said Kate, "did I ever tell you the story of the first time I saw Decker?"

"No, but I'd like to hear about it. You two are so well suited for each other. I'm surprised you aren't a couple."

Both Decker and Kate blushed, suddenly interested in things in the distance. Bridget grinned while they composed themselves.

Kate cleared her throat. "Remember I got chosen for the Pippin Corp panel to test the Pip5?"

Bridget nodded.

"Well, that turned into a disaster because I met my ex-boyfriend, Lucas, there. Don't even want to waste any time talking about that loser. Anyway, when the phone came out, I lined up like the rest of the sheep in Chicago and waited to get my phone. Mine was free because of the panel. Standing in line outside, I noticed some hot guy in spandex shorts cycling by. The first thing I noticed was his smile. Next his legs. Later, when I was inside, he appeared again. I was certain he was looking at me."

Decker met Kate's eyes. "I was."

Kate gave him a light smirk. "I wanted to talk to him but was too caught up in the excitement of a new phone. I still regret that. But soon after that, the Sleepless epidemic began."

"But we did meet up again AIB," said Decker.

"Yes, we did. We ran into each other in North City. He reminded me where we'd met, and we struck up a friendship. I didn't have the energy for a romantic relationship. That was ten years ago." She kicked a pebble off to the side and mumbled, "Too late to do anything about it now."

"Kate, don't say that!" said Bridget. "It's rare to meet someone you connect with. I've met two men in my life that I felt a strong connection to. Your grandfather, Henry, and Desmond. Don't make the mistake I did. I should've stayed in Desmond's camp longer and gotten to know him better." She gripped Kate's shoulder. "It's never too late if it's the right person, young lady."

Decker tried not to feel hopeful, but he found himself wondering if a relationship with Kate really was still possible. He'd been in love with her from that moment he'd spotted her engrossed in her smartphone. He silently thanked Bridget for putting her stamp of approval on one at all.

"Don't embarrass her, Bridget," Decker said, trying to sound casual. Then he added, "But I will say I'm open to becoming more than friends."

Kate laughed. "This really isn't the time or place to talk about this. We're on a rescue mission, remember?"

Decker cleared his throat and made his back ramrod straight. "Yes, of course." He gave her a mock salute. "Lead the way, Commander Kate! If we succeed, may my reward be a date?"

Kate groaned and Bridget giggled. "Yes. First, let's get Stephen, and then we can go on a *date*. Maybe go to the garbage shopping mall? You can find me a present."

"Oh, I forgot, I already *did* go shopping." Decker dug around in his backpack and drew out the MP3 player he'd found on the first day he tried scaling the Wall. "I saw this and thought of you. I completely forgot about it until now."

"That's a sweet gesture," said Bridget. "Isn't it, Kate?"

Kate just smiled, and Decker found himself walking with butterflies in his stomach.

Buildings could be seen in the distance, and the group stopped to take a break. "Should we go over our plan one more time?" asked Bridget.

Decker nodded. "Kate, you first."

"Get a job in the Capital and find out if the president has any plans to go after our group. If I have the time and get lucky, I'll search for documentation about the Sleepless plague."

"Bridget?" Decker asked.

"I'm going to be the lookout once you discover where Stephen is being kept—if he's a prisoner. If he isn't a prisoner, we'll look for him in North City until we find him."

"Right. Okay, you both know what to do. We'll meet up again in one week. Sooner if we get lucky. If Bridget and I get Stephen to come with us, we'll meet you at the ITS. If he refuses, we'll go to the Capital and find you. Any questions?"

They were as ready as they were ever going to be. Decker tried not to lose faith in Stephen. If he'd been fooled by him the entire time he was with the Dreamers, Decker didn't know if he could continue to lead. What kind of leader misjudged a person that badly?

"Okay, everyone onward to the train," said Decker. "Hopefully we'll be on the same one next week with an additional passenger."

CHAPTER ELEVEN

Kate's stop was first. The train slowed and the doors opened.

"I'll see both of you at the end of the week." Her grandmother was frowning. "Don't worry about me, Bridget. I'll be careful." Bridget squeezed her hand tightly before letting her go.

Kate could feel the eyes of Decker and Bridget on her as she walked away. She turned around to confirm it. Waving and smiling to put them at ease, Kate then continued on her journey to the Great Hall. She wasn't looking forward to seeing the building again.

Be brave, Kate.

She arrived at the familiar building, her anxiety building as she drew closer. This was where she'd had to come to be assigned tasks, usually the task she hated most of all—cleanup. Before she met Decker, she'd had to do those alone. A shudder passed through her as she remembered the broken bodies of the young ones who'd fought for the glory of their sectors. Glory. What a crock. She entered the hall and looked over at the task line. As expected, there was Pete, the one worker who gave her the creeps and always teased her.

Kate stood in the back of the long line. To pass the time, she rehearsed the story she'd tell Pete when she got to the front. She vowed not to make eye contact with the lecherous old man. In the past, he'd made comments about her appearance and alluded to his desire to go out with her. Due to her desperation back then, she'd had to listen and smile. She struggled every time not to tell him what an asshole he was.

Finally, it was her turn. She stepped to the window, trying to look forlorn and downtrodden.

A sneer broke out across his face. "Well, well, well, it's Curly. Haven't seen you around here for a few weeks. Where have you been?"

"Oh, um ... I've been around. I think I came in when you weren't working."

Pete looked at Kate with suspicion. She could tell he was trying to determine if she was lying.

"Well, whatever. A shame, though. I missed seeing your beautiful eyes." Peter reached over and stroked her face. "And your lovely, curly red hair."

Revulsion hit Kate. She backed away a couple of inches so he was no longer within touching range. Anger flashed across his face.

You have to do this, Kate. She shook the feeling off and did the exact opposite of what she was feeling—she smiled at him. That seemed to put him at ease.

"So what will it be today, Curly? What type of task are you looking for? I remember you liked those cleanings."

Kate's eyes opened wide with shock, wondering where he got that idea. Was this part of his teasing?

"Not anymore, Pete. Mind if I call you Pete?"

Now it was Pete's turn to be shocked. Kate smiled again, glad she could turn this creep's feelings against him. It was the first time she'd addressed him by his name. She could tell he was a little suspicious, yet excited.

"I want a completely different job this time, Pete. I've heard there are some awesome jobs in the Capital. Can you hook me up with one of those?"

"I could. What's in it for me?"

Crap. "Um ... My undying gratitude?"

Pete coughed. "Uh, yeah, okay. Hmm ... let me look."

Peter swiped his tablet, mumbling to himself. Kate was grateful he hadn't tried to get her to sleep with him. Maybe he was just one of those curmudgeons who was in reality a coward. She didn't plan on staying around to find out.

"Okay. Jobs in the Capital are rare. But this morning a new posting came in. President Grieves is looking for a new aide."

Kate couldn't believe her luck. "Really? I could do that? There's never been a female aide before. She's always been surrounded by men."

He shrugged. "Beats me. Maybe she's sick of them. Don't look a gift horse in the mouth, Curly. You want this or not?"

"Oh, yes! What do I do next?"

Pete gave Kate an address in the city. He said he'd send her name ahead so they'd be expecting her.

"Don't I need some sort of letter?"

"Did I say you needed a letter, Curly?" he barked.

Turns out he really was a jerk.

She jumped on a train at the Intercity Transport Subway. For the first time, she boarded the train to the Capital. The ITS was a leftover from before, and only five lines still worked. One each for the four cities and the one she was on, headed to the Capital. It didn't feel any different from the other ones, yet it was taking her to the one place she'd always said she didn't want to visit.

The advertising signs were the same here. The one that always fascinated her, the one Decker used to steal Somnum for her, was on the opposite wall. If it weren't for Remus, the man who'd posted the signs, she might still be cleaning up after the Sector Series.

NEED BONUS SLEEP? CALL 767VJM.

The train to the Capital was an express, so in a quick fifteen minutes, she arrived. Everything in the Capital was nicer than in North City. Even the escalator in the ITS station worked. Kate wondered if the other cities were like this. Perhaps North City was the worst. Pete had uploaded the map to her flash drive. The address for President Grieves's office was half a mile away. Once there, she looked up at an all-glass skyscraper with an imposing set of double doors. She walked in and told the person at the desk she was expected, then sat and waited.

There was a huge crystal bowl filled with wrapped chocolates on the table in front of her. Tempted to take one, she resisted, although she hadn't tasted chocolate since AIB. Next to the bowl was a pitcher of iced tea with fresh lemon slices floating in it. She resisted that as well. Taking these without being invited felt like some sort of test. Or was she being paranoid?

The door opened, and a man walked out and scanned the waiting room. His eyes rested on the bowl and pitcher. He smiled.

"You must be Kate. I expected someone much older, but oh well, I don't make those kinds of decisions. My name is Frank."

Kate rose and offered her hand.

"Don't bother. You won't be around long enough to warrant a handshake."

That response was unexpected. She pulled her hand back awkwardly. Did he know she was with the Dreamers? *Calm down, Kate, there's no way he knows that.*

"The first step in this process is for me to ask you some questions. If you give me satisfactory answers, you get to speak with President Grieves. If not, you're back to wherever you came from. Back to earning sleep. Ready?"

Stunned, all Kate could do was nod.

"Well then, follow me into the next room and take a seat."

They walked down a long hallway with closed doors on either side. At the sixth door, they entered a small office equipped with a wall of vidscreens. All were off, creating the illusion of a glossy black mirror. He turned suddenly to face her and gave her an intense look.

"Tell me, Kate, why didn't you take any of the chocolates or drink the iced tea?"

"They weren't mine to take. No one offered any to me, so I chose to leave them alone."

"That's an interesting answer. When was the last time you had chocolate?"

"Ten years ago, sir."

A smug little smile appeared. Frank seemed to like being addressed as sir. "If it were me, I would've taken a chocolate, but then, I'm not looking for a job. Follow me."

Frank and Kate went through an interior door to the next office. Kate suppressed her excitement. She'd passed the first test. They waited for a few moments until the next interviewer showed up. He was a short, squat man who fidgeted with his tie as he entered the room.

"This is Gareth," said Frank. "He will be asking you some questions before you move on. Or rather, *if* you move on." With that, he left the room.

This time Kate didn't offer her hand. Instead she stood waiting for instructions.

"Kate, have a seat."

Kate looked for a chair and saw that the only one was in the far corner of the room. She sat on the lumpy cushion and wondered if this was another part of the interview. A *Princess and the Pea* moment.

"I have only one question for you. *Think* before you answer. If I offered you an unlimited supply of Somnum, would you kill someone for me?"

"No."

"That's it? Just no?" Gareth asked.

"I would rather die from lack of sleep than kill someone."

"Okay, then, follow me to the next room."

Kate was surprised he didn't ask anything else. This was the strangest interview she'd ever experienced.

Gareth motioned toward a tall, thin man with regret etched on his face. "This is Roger. You'll be replacing him if the president hires you."

This made Kate feel uneasy. If Roger was going to lose his job because of her, couldn't he just sabotage her interview? Or was he leaving of his own free will? Would anyone leave a job here? She needed to stay alert.

Roger got right to the point. "If the president asked you to kill someone, would you do it?"

"No, I wouldn't," she said quickly. "As much as I would like to follow her orders, that one I would have to refuse."

"Really? This is the president," said Roger. "Why wouldn't you follow her orders? She would be your boss."

"I wouldn't follow that particular order. Anything else, yes, but killing?" Kate shook her head. "I draw the line there. I wouldn't do that for anyone."

"What if it was self-defense? Would you fight back or let them kill you?"

Seriously? Was she going to become some kind of assassin?

"I've had enough of this nonsense, Roger. I've answered your question. Now take me to President Grieves at once and stop asking me the same stupid question over and over. I don't have all day!"

Kate held her breath, hoping her aggressive stance worked. If it didn't, she didn't know what to do next.

"No one talks to me like that!" shouted Roger. He stood up, his face turning bright red. "I'll have you—"

The door opened, and in walked President Grieves.

"You heard her, you idiot! Leave at once. I have my new aide." Grieves flashed a devilish smile at Kate, who had to fight the urge to look away in fear.

A dejected-looking Roger left without complaint. She'd done it. Kate had her Capital job. She felt oddly proud of herself.

"You're pretty confident, aren't you, young lady? I like that, but beware. You're allowed to use that attitude on anyone here except for me. Understood?"

"Yes, President Grieves," said Kate, bowing her head down respectfully. "I would never disrespect you. I want this job because I admire you. Your intelligence, kindness, and natural leadership qualities are what make you a great president."

Kate wanted to choke on the false compliments, but she needed to win over the president now, while she was still new.

Grieves smirked. "You're a smooth bullshitter. I like that. I like you."

"Thank you. I appreciate that. When would you like me to start?"

"Do you live in the Capital?" Grieves asked.

"No, I'm from North City, but I would love to live here."

More lies to swallow, but things were going the way Kate needed them to.

"This position includes housing here in the Capital Building and, of course, unlimited Somnum. You start immediately. Go to my aide Frank with this note." She scribbled something on a notepad and snapped the paper to Kate. "He'll get you set up. I'll see you back here this afternoon."

"Thank you. Thank you so much."

Kate walked back through the two rooms to the original spot Frank first questioned her. She handed him the note and waited.

As he read the note from the president, Frank looked visibly upset. "So you're the new Roger." He sighed. "It is what it is, I suppose. In case no one told you, he was the third aide. In other words, if you mess up, you're out of here. Just like Roger. She wants you to get a suit. Come with me and I'll find something to fit you. We've never had a female aide, so I'll have to find one of the president's old suits."

They climbed three sets of stairs and entered an enormous closet full of women's suits. Frank explained that President Grieves only wore an outfit seven times before it was sent to the discard closet. Kate wondered who was making these beautiful clothes and what the significance of seven was to her.

"Here, try on this one," said Frank, handing her a navy-blue pantsuit.

Kate went around the corner for some privacy and slipped on the suit. Surprised it fit her, she stood in front of the floor-length mirror admiring herself, forgetting about her mission for a brief moment. The clothes, the job, and her new room in the Capital, all of it seduced her. But only for a few minutes. She walked out and showed the suit to Frank, who signaled his approval.

"Pick out four more. The president hates to see anyone wear the same thing two days in a row. If you make it past the first week, you can come back and get more clothes. Now, let me show you to your room. Oh, and don't think I'm now your manservant. I'm doing all of this on her orders. After today, I'm your superior. Got it?"

"Yes, sir. Thank you, Frank."

He furrowed his brow, as if unsure whether she was being sincere. She smiled at him, enjoying the fact that he didn't seem to be able to read her.

When they reached her room, Kate had to fight the urge to gawk like a peasant in a palace. Her room was twice the size of her old pod. The siren call of forgetting about the Dreamers swelled one more time, but then Decker's smiling face and the memory of their promised date flashed in her mind, and the temptation disappeared. All she cared about was finding Stephen and getting back to the others. The Dreamers. Her friends.

Her family.

CHAPTER TWELVE

Once Kate split off from their group, Bridget and Decker were left to explore North City. Bridget had been there a couple times but never for long, so she wasn't as familiar with it as Decker. It felt like a second home to him because of his visits to Kate over the years. Ever since he'd found out what cleanings took out of her, that was how he showed his friendship and love for her. He hated the task, too, but it was worth it to spare her the grief.

When they got to the Great Hall, unbeknownst to Kate, they watched her talking to Pete. While Decker didn't think Kate incapable of carrying out her part of the plan, he couldn't help but feel protective of her. He knew of Pete's history of teasing her and his implied lechery. Thankfully, she got her job without too much trouble.

"It looks like she's just fine, Bridget. Let's get out of here before she sees us."

Both walked out of the hall and headed toward Kate's old pod. She'd given them the code to get in so they would have a place to stay for the next week. Decker keyed in the code, and they entered Kate's old home. Bridget could feel a part of Kate remaining within the walls. Although not an artist, Kate had sketched a picture of her cat, Moongie, and stuck it on the wall. A tiny closet contained a pile of neatly stacked clothes. Her kitchen was clean, the cabinets full of EnUR-G bars. The only thing out of place was Kate's unmade bed.

Bridget went and stood by the bed. "I'm kind of relieved to see that her bed is not made. I was starting to think this wasn't Kate's apartment, Decker. She was always a bit of a slob. It's so strange for me to see things in such neat, orderly piles."

"Really? I thought she was the neat type, but then again, I didn't really know her BIB. We had that one interaction she told you about and that's it. We never saw each other again until after all this madness began."

They put their backpacks in the closet, sat down, and began discussing what they were going to do next.

"I want you to go to the library and see if you can find any records about what happens to people who are arrested in the Nation," Decker said. "I doubt there'll be anything useful, but we need to check wherever we can. Maybe you can strike up a conversation with one of the librarians, feel them out and see if they seem open to talking. Don't make yourself stick out, though, okay?"

"Sounds good to me. What will you be doing while I'm at the library?"

"I'm going back to Pete's pod. We know he's working at the Great Hall right now, so he won't be home. I want to see if there's anything there that could be useful to us." Decker checked the time. "Let's meet back here in two hours. If either of us doesn't show, that means something is wrong. Whoever comes here needs to head back to the ITS station, take the train, and get out of town."

"But what about Kate? We can't leave her behind," said

Bridget, unable to keep the alarm out of her voice. They hadn't discussed this earlier.

"Let me finish," Decker said, holding up a hand. "Whoever takes the ITS will go back to the campground and grab Jeremy, then come back for Kate. Don't worry, I don't plan on either one of us getting caught, but it's always good to have a backup plan."

They left Kate's pod, with Bridget heading to the library and Decker to Pete's pod, both hoping to see each other in two hours.

Decker walked into Kate's pod expecting to see Bridget. The library wasn't far away, so he thought she'd finish first. It took him less than the agreed-upon time to return. Trying not to panic, he sat and waited the fifteen minutes that would bring him to two hours. Three minutes before he had to leave for the ITS, Bridget ran through the door, breathless.

"I'm sorry if I worried you. I was having an interesting conversation with the librarians."

"It's okay. I mean, I was just about to leave, but you're here now."

"Anyway, they showed me the tablets the Sector Series contestants write their farewell letters in. Did you know they did this?"

"No, but it sounds sad. Did you read the letters?"

"Yes, I read every letter." Bridget's shoulders slumped. "I'm a wreck right now. The librarians also shared some gossip with me. I'm not sure why we bonded, but we did. They told me there are rumors going around about a factory at the edge of the Capital. When I hinted that I was looking for someone, they suggested we look there."

"This information is great. It's good you stayed to get it."

"Did you find out anything at Pete's pod?"

"Not a thing. It doesn't matter now, though. We need to get on a train to the Capital right away and find this factory. Right now that's our best bet in finding Stephen."

Riding the escalator out of the ITS station, Decker and Bridget were amazed at the difference between North City and the Capital. The Capital station was clean, everything worked, and the passengers were better dressed. It was the first time either of them had visited the Capital. It was like another world.

Neither spoke on the train. Now they continued to travel in silence. Decker assumed Bridget was as surprised as he was by their surroundings. At the top of the escalator was a map of the city. He'd hoped there would be an icon marked 'factory' on it, but he quickly realized the futility of that wish. If the factory was a secret, it wouldn't be advertised anywhere.

"If you were building a secret factory, where would you put it?" asked Decker.

Bridget scanned the map, looking for clues.

"I'd build it close to the ITS so that whatever I was manufacturing would be easy to transport. Also, I'd have some kind of barrier hiding my building from prying eyes like ours."

She looked around and then pointed to an area on the map next to a wooded area that matched all her conditions. Of course, the wooded area showed no factory, but it was still a good location.

"Asking around would probably get us arrested, so I think we should just explore the area you chose. It makes sense to me, and we have to start somewhere. It's as good a place as any."

"If we're here more than one night, I can show you the

best places to sleep at the ITS station," said Bridget. "They all have similar floor plans, so I can find us a hidden spot."

The area they were looking for was only a couple of miles from the ITS station. When they got to the outskirts of the woods, they both checked to see that they weren't being watched, then proceeded. The trees were close together but not impossible to pass. Eventually they got through, and to his surprise they found a chain-link fence surrounding an enormous concrete-block building.

"Bridget, did you have one of your feelings about this or was it just a lucky guess?"

"I didn't even think about trying to feel anything. I used logic in this case." She winked at him. "Glad to know that still works."

"Well, this is as good a spot as any to look for Stephen. I have a feeling that rat Remus turned him in as soon as they arrived in the Capital. Once he got here, there was no reason for him to keep Stephen by his side."

"I think you're right." She huffed, clearly annoyed thinking about Remus. "So what do you think is the best way to sneak into the building?"

"We have to wait for nightfall, and then we'll see. We can spend the daylight hours walking the perimeter and see if there are any openings. If not, then tonight we'll climb the fence. We're lucky there's no barbed wire at the top. Once we're on the other side, we can start looking in windows. If we can't see anything, then we'll camp somewhere inside the fence and start looking in the morning. What do you think about that?"

"That's a grand plan. Let's do it."

They walked around the perimeter of the building, examining the fence for any weak spots, but unfortunately for them, there were none. Still, Decker was glad there were no guards patrolling outside. The fence was strong, and it didn't look like anyone had ever attempted to cut through it. With no visible way in, there was nothing to do but wait until nightfall to lessen the chances of being spotted while climbing the fence.

"Decker, I think we should climb the fence near the entrance because there seem to be more windows on the front of the building than in the back."

He nodded. Bridget led the way, climbing with very little effort. Once over the fence, they moved quietly toward the front door, looking for any exterior cameras. As far as he could tell, there weren't any, which Decker found curious. Perhaps they hadn't had a problem with people trying to break in or out? That worried him even more. What were they doing to the workers that kept them from trying to escape? They looked in the first window, but all they could see was a darkened front office with an empty desk.

Moving along the west side of the building, they looked into each window. They saw a cafeteria and hallway that led to several doors. And then the windows stopped. Decker guessed this was where the manufacturing occurred. They walked around to the other side to where the windows began again, and this time they could see into dorm rooms. Most of the occupants had their shades drawn, but there were a few that had their shades up.

In each room, they saw a lone person in a tiny little space, asleep. There were no decorations on the walls; it was a spare, depressing room. When they approached the tenth window, they looked in and both gasped.

There he was. Stephen.

"Hey, Boss, what should we do about the intruders?"

Boss was watching Decker and Bridget walk around the factory. What were they doing? He reminded himself to thank the supervisor for suggesting they hide the exterior cameras.

"Let's wait and see what they're about."

"Think they're trying to rescue someone?"

"Doubt it. No one knows we're here, so let's just keep watching. It's possible they accidentally found the factory and are just curious."

Decker rapped on the window, hoping to wake Stephen. It worked. Stephen opened his eyes and looked toward the window. When he realized what he was seeing, he looked shocked. He jumped out of bed and ran to the window. He looked around for a way to open it and then realized he couldn't. Decker saw the panic in Stephen's eyes.

"It's you!" Stephen put his face up to the window and said, "What are you doing here?" His voice was muffled, but they could understand him.

"We're here to rescue you, Stephen. Are you okay?"

"Does this mean you forgive me? I'm so sorry I was such a fool about—"

At that moment, Stephen's door burst open, and two armed guards stormed in. Before Stephen could say anything else, they shot him, and he fell where he stood.

"No!" Decker screamed. "Stephen!"

Bridget tried to pull him away. "Decker. Decker! We have to go!"

They darted to the fence, climbed over, and sprinted into the woods, not once looking behind them. Not wanting to believe what they had just witnessed.

Not wanting to believe that Stephen was gone.

The ride back to North City was silent again, but for a different reason. Decker felt tears flooding his eyes. He swiped his eyes and replaced his feelings of despair with anger. What just happened? The guards didn't have to kill Stephen. They could have taken him away, punished him, but they didn't have to kill him. And why had no one chased them? Obviously they knew they were there and punished Stephen for it. It just didn't make any sense.

CHAPTER THIRTEEN

Day two of working for the president began early in the morning. There was the staff meeting at 8 a.m., followed by a one-on-one meeting with Glynis. Kate referred to her by her first name in her private thoughts. Unfortunately there wasn't anything of substance discussed in either meeting; it was as if Glynis simply liked to hear herself talk. She also loved to insult her male aides. So far Kate had been spared any barbs.

Then Grieves ordered everyone from the room except for Kate.

"Now that the idiots have left the room, tell me, Kate, why did you want to work for me? You passed the interview beautifully, but you never said anything about your motivation for being here. I saw by your records you've done quite a few of the cleanups. Are you a fan of violence and gore?"

"President Grieves, I'm here because I believe in the Nation and will do whatever it takes to maintain order."

Glynis said nothing, which made Kate nervous. *More, Kate. You have to give her more.* She swallowed the bile rising in her throat. "I see too many of my fellow Sleepless doing nothing to contribute to society. They are leeches and must be whipped into shape. I want to help you enforce your rules and keep things running smoothly."

Glynis smirked. "That's a good answer, although a bit trite, but I believe you. You still haven't answered my question about the cleanups. Not many take on such a harsh task as often as you. I'd like to know why."

"To be honest—"

Glynis held up a finger. "That's what I want from you, honesty."

"Yes, to be honest, I wasn't thrilled about the cleanups. But I knew I'd be bored working a dead-end day-to-day job. I preferred to earn my Somnum in chunks. Besides, I realized it's an honor to clean up after the Sector Series. Whoever thought up the games is brilliant."

"You don't know who thought of them?"

"No, I don't."

The president lifted her chin slightly. "It was my idea, and I must say I'm exceedingly proud of it. Good work, Kate. Go to your desk and learn everything you need to succeed in your new position. Welcome aboard. This should be a good match."

After the day ended, Kate searched the Capital Building for useful information. She wasn't sure what she was looking for, but she peeked in drawers, looked at tablets, and listened at doors. Then, while standing next to a door in what she hoped was a nonchalant manner, she spied Remus coming into the building. Her heart began racing. She had to hide. Remus would tell the president who she was without a thought.

She slipped around a corner so she could see and hear Remus but without him being able to spot her easily. Kate watched him walk up to the president's office and demand that he be seen immediately. Moments later the door opened, and Remus walked in. The reception aide left his desk, which was a great opportunity for Kate to move closer to the door. There was an old dumbwaiter that was no longer being used. By opening it slightly, Kate could see and hear what was going on in the president's office. She hoped she wasn't being set up, but she needed to know what Remus was saying to President Grieves.

"Now that I've delivered a Sleeper to you, what would you like me to do?" Remus asked.

Kate had to suppress a gasp. He had to be talking about Stephen. But what did deliver mean? Where was Stephen?

"Tell me what else you know about the Sleepers," said President Grieves. "Where are they right now, are they planning anything against me, and who is in charge? I know we spoke earlier, but I need to be sure your information is correct and that you aren't forgetting to tell me something."

A flash of annoyance crossed Remus's face, but he quickly hid it.

"The last time we met I thought I told you the leader's name is Decker. He clearly has a hold over the group; they'll do anything he says. As for their location, the best plan would be for me to lead your group there. But if you're planning on leaving me behind again, I can tell you that they're close to the border of East Sector."

"Do you know exactly where, or are you guessing?"

"My intel is based on their location the last time I was with them. As for whether they have a plan against you—not directly. I know they're looking for a way to escape the Nation. That should be considered a threat to you. Am I correct about that?"

Glynis rapped her fingers on her desk. "This is interesting information. No, I won't make the same decision twice, Remus. This time I'd like you to go with the security patrol and lead them to the last spot that you saw this group. These Dreamers."

"May I ask you a question, President Grieves?"

"What is it?"

Remus cleared his throat. "What's going to happen to Stephen? He's not a bad kid."

Kate felt her face flush with anger. Now *he cares about Stephen?*

"Don't worry about him," said the president. "He's in good hands."

Kate heard the aide returning. She moved back. She'd seen and heard enough; it was time to leave. But should she leave the Capital? The news about Stephen was huge, but she was in an amazing position to find out more. Kate felt torn. Should she stay or go?

Hoping the meeting between Remus and President Grieves lasted longer, Kate wandered down the corridor, looking for unlocked offices. She found one, and making sure no one was inside, she entered the room. There wasn't much there except for a couple of tablets. She walked over and turned them on, flipping through one briefly, then the next. To her shock, the second one belonged to Glynis.

It must be her spare. Or perhaps her personal tablet. She swiped through quickly and opened a folder containing numerous files labeled things such as Population Report, Sector Series, and most interestingly, a file named Insurance.

Her mind raced. While Stephen was their mission, this tablet could hold information much more important to the Dreamers. She had to get it back to Decker.

Before leaving the room, she rifled through some drawers, looking for anything else that might be useful. She found no more information, but she found a large bag of chocolates. This time she took them without a second thought. The Dreamers would be happy to see the treats. She grabbed the tablet, stored it inside her satchel, and left the office quickly.

Kate hurried to her room, trying not to look suspicious. She left from a side door and headed toward the ITS station to head back to North City. She was earlier than planned, but with Remus walking around and being so chummy with the president, she didn't feel it was safe to be hanging out there. Hopefully she could find Decker and Bridget quickly, as Grieves was likely to notice her absence soon.

Riding the ITS back to North City, Kate thought one last time about what it would be like to continue to work for the president, wear beautiful clothes, and have an unlimited supply of Somnum. And then she laughed. Her life was far better than that. She got to live with Decker and the rest of the Dreamers, her days spent accomplishing real things and getting to know people better. And she was never really the type to like fancy clothes, and she much preferred wearing her own. And didn't she already get an unlimited supply of Somnum from Decker? What could be better than that?

Walking up the broken escalator in North City, Kate headed for her old pod. She'd given both Decker and Bridget access and knew it was the best place to look for them. When she got to the pod, it was empty, but that didn't worry her. Kate lay down in her messy bed, happy Bridget hadn't made it, pulled up the covers, and thought of Stephen. Where was he? She hoped he was okay, but she was worried by the phrase Remus had used. Delivered. Kate was tempted to take some Somnum so she could take a nap but didn't feel safe enough to do so. She needed to stay sharp until she met up with Decker and Bridget again.

Then she heard the keypad being activated. She sat up, suddenly realizing that maybe it was the president's men come to take her back for questioning. Thankfully, it was Decker and Bridget.

A look of shock flashed across his face. "What are you doing back so early?" He crossed the room quickly and looked her over, making sure she wasn't hurt. "I'm glad you're safe, and I'm happy to see you, but what's wrong?"

Bridget threw her arms around Kate. Decker looked like he wanted to hug Kate but stayed back instead.

"I got a job, a great job, actually. I was one of the president's aides. But then that rat Remus showed up, so I had to leave before he told the president who I was. I couldn't take the chance he'd recognize me."

Decker nodded. "You did the right thing."

Kate shuddered. "The whole Capital scene made me feel uneasy. The president pretended to like me, but I know she was faking it. She gave me the creeps. Her smile isn't genuine. I almost felt like a mouse being played with by a cat. I expected her to pounce any moment. Anyway, that's not the only reason I'm here. Before I left, I found out something interesting. But what about you two? Have you found Stephen yet?"

Decker and Bridget looked at each other. Kate had a sinking feeling in her stomach. "What is it?"

"Why don't you tell us what you found first, honey," Bridget said softly.

"I overheard Remus say he'd 'delivered' Stephen to the president. That was worrying to me. He also gave the location of the Dreamers and told the president we were looking for a way to escape the Nation."

Decker shook his head. "That's what I was afraid of. They'll go after the group. When did he tell her this? When are they coming?"

"It sounded like soon, but I don't have any details because I had to leave. So what about you? I have more to tell you, but I need to hear what you know first."

"We found Stephen on the outskirts of the Capital."

Kate looked shocked. "You were in the Capital?"

"Yes, Bridget got some good information from the librarians. They saved us a lot of time. There's a factory hidden by trees, and unless you knew to look for it, you'd never think it was there. Anyway, we found the building and Stephen."

"Then where is he?" Kate asked.

Decker lowered his gaze. "We found his room, and we tried to talk to him through a window. Before he—well, he apologized and said he regretted leaving us."

"So how are we getting him out?"

Kate wondered why Decker couldn't meet her eyes. He looked nervous and upset. Her stomach churned as a feeling of dread began to form.

"Guards stormed into the room and he ... he was shot and killed. We couldn't stay. There was nothing we could do for him; we had to escape. We were lucky the guards didn't chase us. I'm still wondering why they didn't. The building he was being kept in was a huge cement thing. It looked like some sort of factory, but neither of us could figure out what they made there. There were no bars on the windows, but it was definitely a prison of some sort."

Kate's whole body slumped, and she felt tears welling in her eyes. Their mission to rescue him was a failure. "I suppose I should tell you what else I found. In an open office, I saw two tablets. One belonged to Glynis."

"Who?" asked Bridget.

"That's the president's first name. Anyway, I looked, and there's an intriguing file loaded called Insurance. I stole the tablet in the hopes that Jeremy will be able to hack in and tell us what's in the file."

Decker nodded. "If anyone can do it, it's Jeremy. But why should the president have a file called Insurance? Unless ... No, we're better off if we wait for Jeremy rather than come up with some crazy theory."

"Well, at least this mission wasn't a total loss," said Bridget. "I still can't believe Stephen's gone, but at least his death was quick, and he did get a chance to tell us he was sorry. So even though we'll bring sad news back, we also bring important news." Bridget gripped Kate's arm and squeezed. "We have more information about what the president is doing, which should help us protect ourselves, don't you think?"

Kate loved the practical side of her grandmother. Already looking for the silver lining.

"I'm ready to go back," said Decker. "Is there anything else we need to do before we leave this awful city?"

"Not a thing," said Bridget. "Let's go."

Kate nodded. "I agree, let's get out of here."

CHAPTER FOURTEEN

On the train from North City, the three of them talked about how to give the bad news about Stephen's death to the Dreamers. Decker argued that he should be the one, and he was determined to win this argument. Bridget said she wouldn't mind doing it because she wasn't the type to get emotional. Kate offered to take the burden from both of them.

"This is not up for discussion, you two," said Decker. "I am the leader and therefore it should come from me. I started this rescue mission, and I need to end it. Don't worry, it's going to be fine. Like Bridget said, we're going back with information that will help all of us."

The walk back to their camp gave Decker, Bridget, and Kate time to sort through their feelings and prepare for what was ahead. Despite his insistence, Decker wasn't looking forward to delivering the news about Stephen. He almost decided to lie and say they didn't find him at all, but he knew he couldn't do that. Lying didn't come naturally to him. He'd slip up and then lose the trust of the group.

"Do you think Claudia and Jeremy were able to take care of things while we were away?" Bridget asked.

"I have complete faith in their abilities. Plus, I had an ulterior motive when I asked them to co-lead the Dreamers. It's time they talk to each other." He smiled slightly. "Jeremy has feelings for Claudia, and it's time he opened up and said something to her. My hope is that he did while we were gone."

Kate laughed. "That reminds me, we've got a date, don't we, Decker? Since you gave me my new MP3 player, we'll have to go shopping for something else at the Wall."

Decker smiled at her, glad that she'd remembered.

"There's the camp," said Bridget, pointing. "Are we ready?"

The three joined hands and walked into the camp, walking in as the group sat down for dinner, and they were met with looks and cries of excitement. But almost at once there were looks of confusion when everyone realized there were only three of them.

"Where's Stephen?" Jeremy asked.

"Well, I believe in tempering bad news with good news, so let's go with the good news first," said Decker. "We found Stephen in the Capital."

The Dreamers cheered. Decker's heart sank. *I've made things worse. Now when I give them the bad news, it'll be harder on them.*

He cleared his throat. "It was just as we thought. Remus somehow convinced Stephen to leave us. He helped that scum escape. But as Kate found out, once they arrived at the Capital, Remus turned him in to the president, and Stephen was taken away to a factory on the outskirts of the city. I don't know the details of how he convinced him or what happened once they got to the Capital, all that I know is the poor guy was sent away."

"What kind of factory?" asked Jeremy. "There's no manufacturing in the Nation other than the crappy clothes we wear. Could it have been that?"

Decker opened his mouth, but Jeremy stopped him. "No, wait, that can't be right. I know where that factory is. That's where Aidan and I stole clothes and shoes for us. What on earth could they be manufacturing?"

"We never found that out either," said Decker. "I have no idea what they're making, but I do know that it was also a sort of prison. It was weird. There's a chain-link fence all around the building. When Bridget and I got there, we looked in the windows until we found Stephen. He was asleep in a tiny little room. We knocked on the window and he came over. He was thrilled to see us. We asked him to come back with us and he said yes and apologized for helping Remus escape."

"Well, what happened? Where is he?" Claudia asked.

Several of the Dreamers asked the same question.

"That's where the bad news comes in, everyone. As soon as Stephen apologized to us, two guards broke into his room and shot him. We had to escape and leave his body behind. The look on Stephen's face when he was shot is something I'll never forget."

No one spoke, the shock and sadness overcoming the Dreamers. Some cried, others stared off into the woods. Decker let the group grieve for several minutes before continuing. He had the urge to cry with them but resisted.

"We do have more good news. Kate managed to steal one of President Grieves's tablets. There's a locked file I'd like to have Jeremy open." He looked at Jeremy. "You up for it?"

Jeremy's face brightened a little. "Yeah. I haven't hacked into a file for ages. It shouldn't take me long."

Kate took it out of her pack.

"I didn't get a chance to look at it much, but I couldn't open the file."

Jeremy turned the tablet on. "I doubt she or her aides are very techno-savvy. What's the name of the file?"

"Insurance. Weird, right?" said Decker.

Jeremy nodded as he flicked through the tablet.

"Kate, why don't you tell him about the conversation you overheard?"

"I tried to listen at doors to get useful information after my work day. At one point, I saw Remus enter the president's office. I hid so he wouldn't see me, but I was able to get close to the door. He told her all about us. Our location, our plans to look for the door. Everything. That rat is as bad as we'd imagined."

Jeremy looked up in alarm. "So that means—"

Decker nodded. "It's time to head out again. I think we switch directions and go west. The security patrol will look for us here, so we're better off going in the opposite direction. We don't have the luxury of waiting. We'll start packing now, even though it's late. We'll travel until nightfall and then set up a temporary camp in the woods rather than by the Wall. Any objections?"

There were none. They were in danger, and they all started dispersing.

Decker turned to Jeremy and Claudia. "Anything happen here I should know about?"

"Nope, nothing noteworthy," said Jeremy.

"Okay. Let's get moving. I have to go talk to Arlene."

He found her helping someone break down their tent. "Hey, Arlene, got a minute?"

"Sure, Decker."

They moved off to the side. "I suggest you and your group come with us," he said. "President Grieves's goons aren't going to care which group of Sleepers you belong to. Will you join us?"

"I was hoping you'd ask. And if you didn't, I was going to. Yes, we'll come with you. I'll get us packed up and get back here ASAP."

"Good. Let's plan to meet back here in two hours. That should give you time to talk to your group and pack."

"Good idea," said Arlene. "The sooner we're far from this camp, the better."

By the time the Dreamers found a safe spot to set up a temporary camp, it was almost midnight. Everyone fell into their sleeping bags, exhausted from the hike and the emotional drain of finding out about Stephen's death. The only two Dreamers still awake were Decker and Jeremy.

"Are you too tired to hack into the tablet?" Decker asked.

"Yes, I'm tired, but this is important." He pulled it out again. "Give me a few minutes."

Decker watched Jeremy work, confident he could do it. A couple of minutes later, Jeremy's expression changed from focused to shocked.

"What? What is it?" He didn't like the way Jeremy was staring at the tablet.

"I think you'd better read this yourself." He turned it and handed it to Decker.

Meeting notes:

- Worried about Russian aggression, a virus was created by the CDC, to be used in the event of biological warfare.
- An unknown person or persons released the agent into the water supply in the city of Chicago and its

surrounding suburbs. The water was also contaminated in parts of Minnesota, Iowa, and Wisconsin.
- There is no cure yet.
- The CDC, with the approval of the president, made plans for evacuation and cover-up.
- Glynis Grieves agrees to lead the new country to keep the Sleepless away from the rest of the population.

Meeting notes:

- Dr. Annie Beaumont has been working on a cure for ten years with no progress; the project needs more funding.
- There are no theories on why some were not affected by the virus.
- Dr. Annie Beaumont is missing, last seen two weeks ago.
- President Glynis Grieves testifies at committee in Washington D.C. for the tenth time. The committee granted permission for President Grieves to euthanize the Sleepless.

"Euthanize the Sleepless?" Decker whispered.

"This is insane, Decker," said Jeremy.

"But this says the *government* did this," he said, his voice rising. "Why would she kill people who did nothing? She's crazy!" yelled Decker.

There were stirrings outside the tent as others heard Decker yelling. He lowered his voice and said to Jeremy, "I don't know what to do about this information. Do we tell the others?"

"I don't know, man."

"If it were me, I'd want to know." Decker paused, then shook his head. "Let's get some rest. This will be the last worry-free night for the Dreamers. Let them have good dreams instead of nightmares tonight. In the morning we'll fill them in. How long will the tablet be usable?"

"I checked the specs. This model has a one-year battery, and it has at least nine months left. Once the battery drains, one of us can sneak into the nearest city and recharge it. I doubt we'd need it that long, but we basically don't need to worry about it."

"Fantastic, I have a feeling it will be helpful to us." He patted Jeremy on the shoulder. "Tell no one, and keep that tablet safe. Sleep well, my friend."

"Good morning, Dreamers. We need to have a meeting before we head out again. First, I appreciate all of you being so flexible and getting us packed up tonight in record time. It's amazing what we can do as a team. Jeremy and I stayed up a little later last night so he could try to hack into the president's tablet. He was successful, but what I'm about to tell you is very disturbing. In fact, Marian, I think your children should go back to the tent. I don't think they should hear this."

Marian looked shocked but listened to Decker and ushered her children away, assuring them she'd be right there.

"There was a file named Insurance on the tablet," continued Decker. "It had transcripts of what I suppose were meetings the president attended. I won't go over everything now but I'll give you the essential points."

He stopped, then took a deep breath. He knew the information would hit them hard. "The Sleepless plague was started by the US government. It was intended for our enemies in Russia but somehow got into the water system in Chicago."

The group erupted in shouts and cries. Someone started openly weeping. Decker held his hands up for silence. "At this point, there is no cure. And the most disturbing thing is President Grieves is apparently sick of leading the Nation, and she has gotten permission to euthanize the Sleepless population."

Audible gasps, screams, and stoic looks were among the reactions. Then they started yelling questions.

"Decker, what do we do about this?"

"Does this mean the government will kill us?"

"What should we do? What about my family?"

"I think we need to fight."

"I think we need to hide."

Decker tried to hide his growing panic. He was at a loss as to what to do next other than try to comfort them. *Stop it. Be strong for them.* He raised his hands again for silence. He couldn't let himself be overwhelmed.

"What we're going to do next is pack up and keep moving deeper into the woods, farther away from the Wall. As we walk, we can discuss our options. But for now, the most important thing is to stay ahead of President Grieves's security squadron. Other than that, I'm sorry to say that I have no real answers for you right now."

"But, Decker—"

"Safety first," he said. "Let's move."

Kate caught up to Decker and took his hand. He was startled but was also happy. She smiled up at him.

"Decker, I know you're stressed out right now, so I want to remind you of two things. One, I'm here for you. And two, by heading west, we are getting closer to Desmond. You might get to see him in a few days. Despite the horrible news we got about the president, you should be happy about seeing your grandfather."

He smiled at her optimism. "I didn't think about that. Thank you for reminding me. That does make me happy. Hopefully he has some advice for me. I hate knowing what we know, but to be honest, it means we have to find him and other Sleepers so his group can prepare. We have to spread the word. Maybe we can join forces and come up with a solution, or at least fight against her together."

"I know. All I'm saying is, focus on the good, Decker. We can get through anything together."

Kate squeezed Decker's hand. He squeezed back.

CHAPTER FIFTEEN

The Dreamers walked for hours and finally stopped, needing a break. They found a shady spot, sat down, and took off their backpacks.

"We'll rest up for half an hour," said Decker. "Then we've got to get moving again."

Everyone groaned, but there were no real complaints. Kate knew everyone was afraid but wanted to change the atmosphere. During her ten years living in North City, she got through each day by trying to remember something happy in her life. She thought she'd give that a try with the Dreamers.

She walked into the middle of where everyone was gathered. "Guys, I know we're all feeling pretty down, but hear me out. Tell me about a memory that made you really happy BIB."

But before anyone spoke, there was a rustle in the nearby bushes. The group jumped up, ready to defend themselves. Out walked a middle-aged woman with a backpack. She was all alone and didn't look threatening, so Kate took a step toward her. "Hi there, my name is Kate. Who are you?"

The woman seemed hesitant to identify herself. She looked past Kate and saw the large group of people, which seemed to intimidate her further.

"I'm not here to make any trouble. I'm just hiking around. My name is Annie Beaumont."

"Nice to meet you, Annie. Where are you headed? And I guess I should get this over with: Are you a Sleeper?"

Annie nodded but said nothing.

"Come over and meet the rest of us. Most of them are Sleepers, but I, unfortunately, am not."

When Annie heard Kate describe herself as Sleepless, she looked visibly upset, which Kate found curious.

"You're not a Sleeper?" She dropped her pack to the ground. "I'm so very sorry, Kate. It's all my fault."

Now Kate was confused. How could it be this strange woman's fault? She was about to ask more when she remembered the report on the tablet, which Decker had shown her late last night. And now she realized why the name Annie Beaumont seem so familiar.

Kate couldn't reveal she knew who she was in front of everyone, so she motioned Annie to follow her to the group.

"Hey everyone, this is Annie. She's a Sleeper, and I invited her to come over and have a chat with us. Annie Beaumont, these are the Dreamers."

"Dreamers?"

"Yes, we call ourselves that because we dream of a better tomorrow rather than focusing on the misery that is the life of the Sleepless." Kate shrugged. "And also the misery that is our life, I guess, since we have to hide out in the woods from the government."

"Nice to meet you all," said Annie.

Kate saw the looks on Decker and Jeremy's faces. They knew who she was, too. Kate caught Decker's eye and signaled to him with a slight shake of her head. She hoped he knew Kate meant not to confront Annie at this point. They needed to think about this first.

"So where are you coming from, Annie?" Claudia asked.

"I was just visiting in South City and then decided to come out in the woods and see how beautiful everything is."

Kate knew she was lying, and apparently so did others.

"Seriously? You wanted to see how *beautiful* everything is?" asked Jeremy. "How do we know you're telling the truth? If you're a Sleeper, why were you still in the city? Everyone knows Sleepers disappear. Or were you hiding your status from the government?"

Annie looked stricken. Her confusion at the statement seemed genuine. "Disappear? Sleepers are disappearing from the cities?"

Jeremy rolled his eyes. He leaned over and whispered something to Decker.

"Yes, they are, Annie," said Decker. "And it seems strange you don't know about that. Every Sleeper I've ever met is aware of the disappearances. That's why we live in the woods. So how about telling us who you really are?"

Kate was ready to tell Dr. Beaumont they already knew, but she let Decker take the lead. She figured out he had a reason for pretending not to know.

"That's a, uh, complicated answer. My name is Dr. Annie Beaumont. Up until two weeks ago, I worked at the Centers for Disease Control in Atlanta."

The group started talking all at once.

"Let her speak," said Decker.

Annie continued. "One day I couldn't take it anymore, and I walked out. I didn't tell anyone I was leaving, I simply walked out and took a flight to Chicago. I needed to see for myself what was going on in the Nation."

Kate fumed, unable to contain her anger now. "Tell them why you needed to see what was going on."

Annie looked startled, but she kept talking. "I needed to be here for two reasons. For years I've carried around an enormous amount of guilt. I ... I was one of the creators of the virus that caused the Sleepless plague."

There were outraged cries from the Dreamers.

"How could you work on such a project?" asked Jeremy. "Didn't you realize you'd be hurting people in your own country?"

"No, I didn't. This virus was meant to be used on our enemies. Even that fact bothered me, but you don't understand how long I've been with the CDC. I've always worked on projects that I thought would have good outcomes. Vaccinations, cures for diseases, finding the source of an epidemic."

Annie took a deep breath and continued.

"This is the first time they asked me to do something that I had moral objections to. The only way I got through it was thinking that this would stop an enemy of our country, that I could save people *here*, even if it meant harming others elsewhere. But what we didn't predict was that someone would steal the virus and drop it into the water source. I tell myself all the time that I couldn't have known, but I feel extremely guilty about all of it."

"And what's the second reason?" Bridget asked.

She looked at Bridget, hope springing to her face. "I've been working for ten years trying to figure out how to reverse the effects of this. I've gotten close a few times but still no cure." She looked down. "I don't know that there will ever be a cure, and that makes me feel even worse."

"You should. Do you have any idea what it's like in here?"

Annie looked distraught. "No. But my motivation for coming here was to try to warn the Sleepless that President Grieves has a terrible, horrible plan for them. But when I got to North City, I didn't even know where to start. I didn't want to go up to a random person and say, 'Hey, the president wants to kill you. Where can I find her?' They'd lock me up for being a crazy person. Or have me killed."

"Wait, how did you get in?" asked Decker.

"Through the south door."

"So the rumors are true! Thank you for confirming that for us," said Arlene.

"Kate, Arlene, and Bridget, let's talk to Annie in private for a bit," said Decker while motioning them toward a thicket of trees.

"We're aware of President Grieves's plan," said Decker. "I won't go into all the details, but we're on the run from her security squad. We're being chased and need to find other Sleepers to help us."

Annie looked relieved, and Kate was sure that Dr. Beaumont would join them and help. She looked over at Bridget for confirmation and was met with a smile. And then the implications of what Annie said hit her fully. She was a person from the outside world!

"I'm not the enemy," Annie was saying. "I finally left my job after hearing about the president's insane solution for disbanding the Nation. I want to help you and the Sleepless."

"Why should we trust you?" said Aidan.

"I left my teenager behind with my mother," said Annie. "My husband divorced me because I wouldn't let this go. There's no one at home. Let me come along."

"We need to go, so we'll have to trust you for now, Dr. Beaumont," said Decker. "But know this: We'll be watching you until we know you can be trusted. You stay where we can see you at all times. And no going off without telling us."

Annie nodded. "Fair enough. Where are we going?"

"We're going to continue walking west," said Decker, "and hopefully the squad will continue looking for us in the east. There's a group of Sleepers we're looking for."

"All right." She hefted her backpack on. "Lead the way."

As they continued their journey west, Kate could see Decker was getting nervous. She pulled him aside to talk to him.

"Excited about seeing your grandfather again?"

"I am, but for some reason the thought of seeing him after ten years makes me nervous. I want him to be proud of me."

"Why wouldn't he be proud, Decker? You're being silly." She took his hand, and they walked together, both feeling a bit lighter in their step but still deep in thought.

They arrived on the outskirts of a camp in the late afternoon. Bridget looked around and confirmed it was the last place she'd seen them. She volunteered to go ahead and tell them about their arrival, and Decker said okay, though he was on pins and needles the entire time she was gone.

She returned thirty minutes later with Desmond, who was searching the crowd for Decker. Kate could see how nervous Decker was, and her heart went out to him.

Desmond ran to his grandson and hugged him off the ground, swinging him around like a little boy. The Dreamers cheered. Desmond's Sleepers arrived moments later. Kate smiled at the joyful reunion, tears filling her eyes when Decker's face split into a huge grin.

"I never thought I'd see you again," said Desmond, his eyes wet with tears. "Bridget told me you were a Sleeper!"

"I know. She feels terrible about making that mistake." Decker smiled ear to ear. "You look terrific, Grandpa. I missed you!"

"You're old enough to call me by my name. Come on, everyone. Follow me to my encampment so we can get to know each other!"

The Dreamers met Desmond's group and bonded almost at once. Their common experiences gave them lots to talk about. An older woman walked over to Bridget and gave her a hug. Kate wondered who it was.

"Abigail!" cried Bridget. "I thought I'd never see you again. Look, that's my Kate! I finally found my granddaughter."

"You did?" Abigail smiled. "How?"

"I'll tell you all about it later." Bridget waved Kate over. "Kate, come over here."

Kate walked over. "Hi."

"Hello there, Kate, my name is Abigail. I don't know if your grandmother has told you about me yet. We became close friends when she lived with us. I only wish she'd stayed longer. But I guess if she did, she might not have found you, dear."

"Ohh, Abigail. Bridget mentioned you to me with much fondness. She's told me all about your group. I'm amazed you've all stayed together for ten years. That's a long time."

"That's thanks to Desmond. He's gotten us from the first weeks of chaos to what is now a sense of community and in a lot of ways, calm. We all love him."

Decker was pulling Desmond to the edge of the crowd of Sleepers and Dreamers. Kate knew he was about to make a speech.

"Everyone, quiet down, please. I want to introduce you to someone special. Dreamers, this is Desmond, my grandfather. He is one of the reasons I am the man I am today. Please show him the love and respect he deserves. I concede my place as leader to him if he agrees to join forces with us."

This development surprised Kate. *Maybe it's his emotions speaking.*

"Hello, Dreamers. And no, Decker, I will not accept the

leadership of your group. Don't turn into a slacker, young man. We will co-lead. And yes, I think joining forces is a smart idea. And I don't think anyone would object if I said we'd be honored to be called Dreamers as well. Am I right?"

Both groups seemed excited, and there was a cheer from Desmond's Sleepers.

Desmond motioned for Decker to follow him away from the group.

"Where is Kate? Bridget's told me so much about her." He winked at Decker. "I need to meet her so I can give her my official grandfather's approval."

Kate was nervous. Desmond seemed like a great guy, but what if he didn't like her? Would that sway Decker? Now that they were together, she wanted nothing to get in the way. She walked up to them.

"Well, hello, young lady. I already know all about you thanks to Bridget. I just wanted an excuse to hug you and welcome you to our family. I'm truly sorry about the struggles you've gone through as one of the Sleepless."

She was speechless for a few moments, and then she finally found the words.

"Decker is a lucky guy to have you back in his life," she said. "He never spoke of you very often because it was too painful for him. But I know he thought about you all the time. As he said, you made him who he is. I want you to know that Decker is the reason I didn't suffer as much as I could have. He volunteered to do the worst jobs for me so I could earn Somnum."

"We will do whatever we can to alleviate your pain. If we can't find a cure, then we'll make sure you never run out of Somnum."

Kate smiled. "Now I know why Decker is the way he is. If it weren't for him, I honestly don't think I would have been able to go on." She turned to Decker. "The men in your family are heroes."

Desmond laughed easily. "Heroes, eh? I like you already."

Kate gave Desmond another hug, confident they'd be friends for life.

CHAPTER SIXTEEN

Remus felt vindicated at last. Now that he was assigned to D Squad, he meant to take full advantage of it. The president had hinted he might even be in charge of D or another squad, if all went well. But first he had to find the damned Sleepers. Once they were arrested, his life would improve dramatically.

"The president ordered me to follow you because you are in possession of some important knowledge—the last whereabouts of the Sleepers," said Sergeant Grater. "However, that doesn't mean you're in charge of me or the squad. Got that, Remus?"

"Yes, sir, message received. I wouldn't try to steal your command."

Yet.

The squad boarded a train—their jeeps had long ago fallen into disrepair—at the ITS station headed to East City after each of them got an injector of ViGor from the familiar bright neon machine at the terminal. All the ViGor vending machines had photos of energetic workers adorning the dispenser of false energy. Another useful product from Pippin

Corp. They knew they were in for a long hike and needed the extra boost.

Remus couldn't believe that the government didn't supply their ViGor. He was made to spend his own credits, and he decided that when he was in charge of a squad, he'd demand the president pay. Once he caught the Sleepers, he knew he'd be able to demand a lot of things. His mental list of demands grew.

Remus smiled when he saw one of his old signs still posted in the train.

NEED BONUS SLEEP? CALL 767VJM.

He lost himself in his thoughts about the business he no longer took part in. He didn't miss the work, but he sure missed the bonuses. Whenever he sold black market Somnum to women, he charged extra. Then he frowned. That was why Pete had severed their business relationship. *Uptight bastard.* No matter. Remus would get even with him, too.

He found himself thinking about the ways he could get revenge on Pete, but part of him realized he was angry because he missed having a friend. In all of North City, Pete was the closest thing to one. Remus knew he'd messed up, but he had a hard time admitting when he was wrong. It was Pete's fault anyway, for thinking they were anything close to upstanding citizens. Yet when Pete caught him and cut him off, he wasn't surprised. He'd gone too far and knew he could never patch things up with him.

Who needed friendship, anyway? He had a new goal now: power. Spying on the Sleepers and reporting them to President Grieves had given him a rush he wouldn't soon forget. He was jealous that they could sleep, but when he thought about it, he didn't really have anything against them. And in a way, he respected Decker but would never tell him or anyone else that. Remus wished his life had gone in a different direction, but he also wasn't the type of person who dwelled on the past. Onward and upward to power in the Capital. And favor with the president.

"This is our stop," said Sergeant Grater.

The twelve-member squad ran up the steps and out into the station in formation. It was the last stop for the ITS, but getting to the woods took thirty minutes of jogging. At the end of the half hour, Remus had to ask for the group to slow down. His face warmed when he heard the privates snickering at his lack of physical fitness.

Bunch of muscle-bound idiots. Screw 'em.

Once they entered the woods, Sergeant Grater turned to Remus. "Okay, which way?"

"That way," he said, pointing. "It's about three hours to get there at a brisk clip."

Remus already knew the Sleepers would be long gone, but he didn't want to tell the rest of the squad. It would simply be their starting point. From there, he would decide which direction to go. It felt good to have the other eleven lined up behind him. Pretending he was the leader, he stuck out his barrel chest and tried to be taller. Remus thought power must look good on him.

As he predicted, the Sleepers had moved on. Remus tried to look surprised and swore in mock annoyance. There was no trace of a camp, and if he hadn't recognized the place they'd had him tied to, Remus would've thought he made a mistake. But there was no forgetting the rusted refrigerator that served as his guard when no one was around. He'd been tied to it and ignored except for mealtime. He went over to the refrigerator and shot it.

"What the hell was that for?" shouted the sergeant.

"It's personal, sir. I don't think you'd understand. Anyway, Sleepers are obviously gone. If I remember correctly, their leader, Decker, said they were heading to the East Sector. I suggest we go that way. If that's okay with you, sir."

The sergeant nodded. "Okay, we have a few hours of daylight left. Everyone follow Remus. Keep a lookout for Sleepers and for a place for us to camp. No one leave the group. Got that?"

"Sir, yes, sir," they answered in unison.

"What are the Sleepers like?" asked Sergeant Grater. "I've never met any. Or at least I've never had someone tell me they were a Sleeper."

"They're nothing special. The worst thing about them is they think they're better than the rest of us. Especially their leader. He named his group the Dreamers." Remus snorted. "What a conceited jerk."

"Dreamers, huh? Well, they're special enough to avoid being captured. I wonder if their leader has some military training."

Remus shrugged. What did that matter?

"You better hope you're right about going east, Remus. If not, President Grieves will not be pleased. In fact, maybe I should radio back and tell her we've missed the Sleepers." Grater grinned at him maliciously.

"I'm right. Be patient. If you call her now, she'll only yell and tell us to come back. No, when we find them, it's going to be glorious. She'll probably promote both of us, sir. This could be a good career move."

Graver eyed him suspiciously.

"Tell you what," said Remus. "If we don't find them in two days, give her a call. I'll even talk to her myself. But if we do find them, hands off Decker." Remus glowered. "He's all mine."

"What's your beef with this Decker?"

"I want to wipe that smug grin off his face with my fists. That S.O.B. doesn't have a heart. Left me tied up like a dog. A dog! Maybe I'll do the same to him."

They packed up and continued their hunt for the Sleepers, heading toward East Sector. The rest of the squad grumbled, some of them rumbling about how worthless Remus's intel was. He didn't care. They would see.

"Hey, where the hell are we?" said a private named Anderson. "We've been walking for hours, and the scenery looks the same. Are we going in circles? Sarge, why you letting this amateur lead us?"

Remus stared at Private Anderson. *Pompous little jerk.* From the onset of the mission, he and the others had tried to undermine Remus. Now he was being bolder about it.

Before the sergeant could say anything, another private spoke up.

"Yeah, Sarge. This is ridiculous. Who the hell is this Remus guy, anyway? I ain't following him no more."

"Everyone settle down," said Graver. "I told you at the beginning of this mission I'm still in charge. Remus is leading us to the Sleepers, but he isn't leading us. Thought I made that clear to you knuckleheads." He turned to Remus. "That said, we do seem to be walking in circles. What's going on?"

Remus felt himself starting to sweat. "Sir, the terrain here is similar. You might think I've gotten us lost, but you'd be mistaken. I have a natural sense of direction, and I know we're headed due east."

"Oh yeah?" said Private Rossi. "You using a compass? Because mine says we're heading west, smart guy."

Shit. How do I spin this?

"Of course we're walking west now. There was a dangerous section of the woods I wanted us to avoid. Now that we've done that, we can go east again. Would you feel better if I put you in charge of the compass, Rossi? With Sergeant Grater's permission, of course."

"Whatever," said Grater. "We'll keep going until sunset. Hopefully we find them before we have to camp again."

But as the sun was going down, Remus changed his story.

"Well, they've eluded us again. See those broken sticks over there? They used to be tent posts for the Sleepers. They broke them up to trick us. Tomorrow morning we'll continue through the East Sector and hope we catch up to them."

Remus loved lying. He was a psychopath who cared more about the game rather than the consequences. This had gotten him in trouble before and probably would again, but he didn't care.

"Everyone shut up, I hear something!" said Remus. "Sarge, tell these idiots to shut their mouths!"

Moments later, a rabbit came out of the brush.

"Ooh, a scary bunny rabbit, Remus. Should we shoot it?" asked Private Anderson.

"That's enough, boys," said Graver. "Anyone could have made that mistake, especially a rookie like Remus. Let's keep marching. We can be at the border of East Sector by nightfall if we keep up this pace."

As they marched, Remus looked from side to side, intent on finding some sign of the Sleepers. Although he was lying to the squad, there was a small chance that the Sleepers were actually heading in this direction. He still felt the sting of shame after the two privates complained about his lack of leadership skill. He walked up next to Grater and lowered his voice.

"Sergeant Grater, sir."

"Yes, Remus, what is it?"

"Sir, I think you should reprimand the privates that were being disrespectful to me. If I'm to help this group find the Sleepers, I need to have their respect. And I don't mean leadership. You are the leader, but I'm in charge of finding them, and I need to know that every single one of the members of the squad will do their job, and I don't know that they will if they're not showing me the proper respect."

Let's see what he does with this.

Grater gave him a look but nodded. "You're right. When we camp tonight, I'll have a talk with them." Then he raised a finger in Remus's face. "But they had a good reason for complaining, so watch your back and make sure we are going where we are supposed to be going."

"Absolutely, sir. Why wouldn't I take you to the Sleepers?"

"I have this funny feeling that you don't really know where you're going. I hope I'm wrong."

It would be dark in about an hour, and Remus felt a creeping panic. His reputation was on the line, and if they found no trace of the Sleepers soon, he knew the sergeant and the rest of the squad would turn on him. He didn't want to go back to President Grieves in disgrace. This was his chance to shine, and he refused to screw it up.

"Everyone stop a minute," said Remus. "We're almost to the border between South Sector and East Sector, so we need to make a decision here. Do we go on to the border or do we start looking more carefully around this area, go deeper into the woods, and search?"

Rossi glared at him. "You have no idea what you're doing. First it's the bunnies, and now this."

At that moment, they all heard rustling and looked around at each other. The squad took cover, waiting to see what emerged.

CHAPTER SEVENTEEN

"Frank! Get in here!" said Glynis.

She was furious. A few days ago, her new assistant Kate had disappeared. Today she noticed her personal tablet with her insurance files was missing, too. This was a disaster. She couldn't believe someone had left the door to her other office unlocked. Although she'd only known Kate for a short time, she'd thought she could trust her.

Wrong. The stupid girl must have been a spy for the Sleepers.

Glynis wondered if her ability to read a person was slipping; she hadn't been wrong about someone for a long time. It must be the stress of dealing with the Nation. It was wearing her down.

Frank stepped in. "President Grieves? What is it you require?"

"What is it I require?" she said, her voice rising in pitch. "What is it I require? To not be surrounded by idiots! You interviewed Kate. Didn't you vet her first?"

"I—"

"I'd assumed you had a background check done. How did

you let a spy and a thief into my office? She could ruin everything for me." She rose from her desk. "Get out."

Glynis walked to the window. She needed to take care of this. If she didn't hear from Sergeant Grater by tomorrow, she would take action. Until then, she continued with her day, not letting any of her staff other than Frank know that something was wrong.

She knew what she had to do. She had to find the Sleepers herself. D Squad hadn't reported back yet, which was concerning. No news was bad news. She summoned Sergeant Cramer, leader of A Squad. It was her premier security force and the one she should have sent out to begin with. Another mistake. Cramer entered, and she gave him his task.

"One more thing. I'm going with you, Cramer."

He couldn't hide the shock from his face. "Is that a good—"

"In my life BIB, I fired a gun and took self-defense classes. I won't slow you or your squad down. This problem needs to be solved immediately. I'm tired of incompetence; it ends now. Be ready to go in an hour."

"Yes, President Grieves. The squad and I are always ready. We'll wait in front of the Capital Building for you. Is there any special equipment you'd like us to bring?"

"Now that you mention it, yes. Night-vision goggles. We can't let the dark stop us from looking."

"Looking for who or what, President Grieves?"

"What I'm about to tell you is not for anyone else's ears. Only you and your squad. If this information leaks I'll know it was you and have you executed. Understood, Sergeant Cramer?"

"I promise I will be discreet."

"It's been known to me for quite some time that there are groups of Sleepers hiding out in the woods outside the four cities. Prior to now it hadn't been important enough for me to look for them. There's never been a shortage of workers for the factory because there are Sleepers who continue to live in the cities, and eventually we discover them. But recently I was given information that one of the groups is trying to escape. By escape, I mean they're trying to leave the Nation."

Glynis put up her hand to stop Sergeant Cramer from asking any questions.

"If they manage to escape, they will unwittingly ruin a plan that I have in place. Don't ask me any questions about where they'd go if they escape or any of that nonsense. I don't have patience or time for that right now. Just know that if they escape it's a very bad thing.

"Our mission is to find them and bring them back into the Capital and send them off to the factory. And if they give us any trouble, I give you and everyone in your squad permission to shoot them."

"Are you sure about that?"

"Of course I'm sure. I don't issue orders like that for the fun of it. In fact, that might be the easiest solution. We'll see what happens when we find them. And know this: We will find them."

"Yes, ma'am. I didn't mean to question your authority."

"I'll be outside as soon as possible. Prepare your men, but give them just a brief amount of information, and make sure they understand the importance of this vital mission. You're dismissed."

At the ITS station, A Squad evacuated all citizens from the terminal. Glynis didn't want to share a train with any of the

Sleepless. Their destination was South City. She was smart enough to realize that the Sleepers were looking for the door. It was a secret, but people talked, and if they'd really heard about its existence, that's where they needed to be to protect its secret. The question was, did they know of the exact location? The first goal of their mission was to destroy the door. Then they would head to East Sector if they didn't see them in the south.

It was the first time Glynis had ridden on the ITS. She was disgusted by the dirt on the seats and the garbage on the floors of the cars. Glynis wondered how the citizens put up with such conditions, then realized she didn't care. The rest of A Squad didn't seem to be bothered by the squalor. They were as bad as the rest of the Nation. Moving on with her life once she left the Nation was her top priority.

Departing the ITS station at South City, Glynis was appalled that she had to walk up the escalator. Didn't anyone take care of the infrastructure in this godforsaken place? Then she realized it was her job.

Never mind, it won't matter soon.

"Who knows this area?" she asked.

"I do, President Grieves," said Cramer. "I was on a security tour in the South Sector a couple of years ago. With your permission, I can lead us."

"Excellent. Let's head straight for the Wall. Once we're there, I can get us to our destination with the aid of a compass. You have a compass, correct?"

"Yes, ma'am, it's part of our standard gear. Permission to ask you for clarification."

"Yes, Sergeant, but make it fast."

"Where are we going?"

Grieves smiled. "We're going to a door."

"A door, President Grieves? What door?"

"Don't worry about the details. Just get us to the Wall."

There it was, the Wall. Glynis hadn't been to the Wall for ten years. On her yearly trips to Washington D.C., a helicopter picked her up from the roof of the Capital Building. The closest she'd ever been to the Wall was on the day she took charge of the Nation. She and the rest of her government staff entered via the door in South Sector.

"Sergeant, this is when I need your compass. Set it for the following location: 39.7817° N, 89.6501° W."

He input her coordinates. "All set, President Grieves."

They walked along the Wall until they were at the coordinates she'd requested. Standing in front of the location of the door, she was pleased to see the camouflage was still intact. Vines grew over it, and there was a pile of equipment stacked in front. From this side it would be difficult to notice the door. For anyone entering the Nation, there was just enough room behind the equipment to open the door and enter.

As she turned to address A Squad, Glynis noticed the vines appeared to have been moved recently. Looking closer, she saw shoe prints heading into the Nation. At least they weren't headed out, but she wondered who would come in and not announce themselves. She felt her face growing hot. Someone had entered without telling her. Not being in control infuriated her.

"There doesn't seem to be any sign of the damned Sleepers. Let's destroy this door and look for them in the east. I think shooting the keypad will be enough."

Once the squad disabled the door they returned to Glynis.

"Time to get going." She tossed the compass back to

Cramer. "I won't need it for this portion of the trip. We'll follow the Wall."

They were moving swiftly, hoping to discover the Sleepers. Glynis was ready for this to be over. The footsteps at the southern door were bothering her. Was the U.S. government spying on her? Were they about to go back on their promise?

This is why I need my tablet back. My insurance. She cursed her stupidity for not having a backup.

"Ma'am," said Cramer, "we will not get there tonight. I respectfully suggest we camp and start again early in the morning."

He was right, but Glynis never gave someone else credit for their ideas.

"I was just about to suggest the same, Sergeant. You should have had more faith in my leadership. Do you think I don't know what I'm doing? Maybe being bumped down to a private would teach you some respect!"

Sergeant Cramer looked shocked at her outburst. Glynis loved that look.

"No, President Grieves, I apologize if you thought I was undermining your authority."

"Do not let it happen again."

At sunrise, the group continued their trek to the east. If her calculations were correct, they'd be there by noon. High noon. How fitting. A showdown between her and the Sleepers. They'd better be there. She didn't trust this important mission to any of her squads. Being present was her way of maintaining control of the situation.

Shortly before noon, they passed the door in the east and saw no sign of anyone. No mysterious footprints. Nothing.

Showing disappointment would be weakness, so instead, Glynis yelled.

"Where the hell are these runaways! Keep moving! We won't stop until we find them."

"Our water is running low, ma'am. May we have permission to go into the woods and look for water? It shouldn't take long, but we won't be able to march much longer without it."

"While you're at it, fill my canteen." She tossed it to the sergeant.

She followed them to the edge of the forest and waited. She heard voices that didn't belong to her men. Then silence. She walked over to where she'd heard them and peered out from behind a bush and watched as D Squad ran into the woods. Hiding! They were hiding from her and A Squad. *Idiots!*

She decided to let them suffer until her squad returned from getting water. *This could prove amusing.*

As A Squad returned, they were talking, not being quiet. *Perfect*, she thought.

"Sergeant Grater! Get your cowardly ass out of the bushes!"

She couldn't wait to see the expression on his face. She heard whispering from the woods. Her squad looked confused. She'd only told them to stand down.

"If I have to ask you one more time to come out of the woods, Sergeant Grater, you will be thrown in jail!"

All of D Squad, including Remus, walked out, looking embarrassed. None of them said a word or made eye contact.

"Well? Have you found the Sleepers? Why haven't you called me yet?"

"President Grieves, ma'am," said Remus. "We were waiting until we had good news for you. Didn't want to burden you until then."

"Didn't you think it would be more of a burden if I didn't know what was going on? What's your excuse, Sergeant Grater?"

"I have no excuse, ma'am. I shouldn't have let Remus sway me. My instinct was to call, but I listened to him and changed my mind. Please accept my apology, President Grieves."

"I'll think about it. And why did you and the squad scurry off into the woods when you heard us? I watched, and you looked like a pack of scared children, not a highly trained security squad."

"We have no excuse. I take full responsibility."

"It seems the Sleepers are still at large. I suggest we wait in the woods opposite the door."

"What do—"

"No questions, Sergeant Grater, just listen and do not interrupt. We wait for a day to see if the Sleepers show up. If, after twenty-four hours, they don't, then I think the next step will be to head west. We won't give up until we find them. Understood?"

Both sergeants answered yes.

"Let's settle in and make camp. No one sleeps tonight. I don't want to miss the Sleepers. Now someone get me some food."

The next morning, President Grieves gave up on the east door. Glynis decided the Sleepers didn't know it existed and were not going to show up. She ordered everyone back to the Capital. A few hours after they began their march back, she got a call from Frank.

"President Grieves! There was a sighting of Sleepers in the Capital. I followed them back to the ITS station. There were about ten of them and only me, so I couldn't apprehend them."

"Why didn't you take reinforcements, you idiot!"

"There wasn't time. I would have lost them. But I have good news for you: I saw them board a train for East City."

Glynis told the squads they were heading back to the east door.

CHAPTER EIGHTEEN

The newly formed larger group of Dreamers chattered away like old friends. Decker thought things couldn't get any better. He was reunited with Desmond, and he and Kate were getting closer day by day. But now the next thing on his agenda, the most important thing, was to find the door so they could escape from the Nation. He knew that any day now the president's security squad would find them, and then they would all be arrested. He couldn't let his happiness get in the way of the safety of the Dreamers.

"Hey, everyone, let's settle down for a minute. I think it's wonderful that we're all getting along. Joining our two groups was an excellent decision and I want to thank Desmond for agreeing to that, and for suggesting he and I co-lead. And hey, because I'm still one of the leaders, I get to give orders."

The Dreamers laughed.

"So, Desmond, if you disagree with me, let me know, but I don't think we have the luxury to sit around and talk. We have to pack up your camp and head out. Please only take what's necessary. Then we'll head to the door."

"What door?"

"We don't have time to go into the details right now, but it's been confirmed to us by Annie that there is a door to the outside. You'll have to trust me on this one, Granddad."

Desmond nodded his agreement. It was as simple as that. They were in tune with each other. Decker wanted the next part of the conversation to be private. They moved away from the group and continued talking.

"Decker, do you know where the door is located?" asked Desmond.

"No, I don't. I've only heard rumors, but we have a new member of our group that has to know, because she came from the outside."

Desmond looked shocked. "She came from the *outside*?"

"Yeah, I know it seems impossible. But everything Grieves has ever told us is a lie. The world is still out there, functioning like nothing happened!"

Desmond looked like he was too shocked to say anything, so Decker continued.

"There's more. Essentially, the Sleepless plague was created by our government. Not President Grieves, I'm talking about the U.S. Government. I read about it on a stolen tablet. You'll get a chance to look at it later. But the worst part: President Grieves has permission to euthanize the Sleepers!"

Desmond's frown deepened. "That's a lot to digest. My group and I were at peace with being out here. Our goal has always been to make things better where we were living. We didn't believe there was anything left over there. We've had no plans on the horizon that involved leaving."

"Believe me, it was the same for us."

"I wish I'd had this information sooner. Who is this new member?"

Decker called Annie over.

"Desmond, I'd like to introduce you to Dr. Annie Beaumont."

Annie nodded at Desmond. "Good to meet you, Desmond. I'm not going to waste time mincing words here: I'm one of the people that created the virus that caused this epidemic of sleeplessness."

A dark look crossed Desmond's face. He looked at Decker, who shook his head to tell him to keep listening.

"It wasn't intentional on my part," she insisted, "but there it is. I take responsibility. As for getting into the Nation, Decker's right. There is a door in South Sector that I can lead you all to. I have a special key card to open the door, and there's also keypad. I don't know the combination, as it wasn't necessary since I have the card. So unless anyone has any questions for me, I agree with Decker. We need to get out of here as soon as possible."

The look of shock on Desmond's group matched Decker's when they first heard about where Annie came from and what she'd done. He suggested that Desmond talk to his group privately before they made any decision. She was too important to them now to let anything get in the way.

They agreed to leave within the hour. Frantic packing began while both groups continued to chatter, getting to know one another better. Aidan and Kirsten were working as one, deep in conversation. Kate noticed and couldn't help but smile. Aidan needed someone like Kirsten to heal.

When it was time to go, they gathered around the two leaders, waiting for directions.

"While you were packing, Decker and I discussed the quickest way to get to South Sector," said Desmond. He paused, unsure of how to tell everyone what they were planning. "We're all taking the ITS."

People began protesting immediately.

"Are you insane?"

"How can this be part of our plan?"

"What if we get caught?"

"Hold on. Hold on!" yelled Desmond. "Yes, I know some of you think we've lost our minds, but give us a chance to explain. We are being chased through the woods, right? Where are we not being chased? In the cities."

People mumbled, still not convinced.

"If we board the train in West City for South City, there's only one transfer in the Capital," said Decker. "The platforms are next to each other, so it should be simple."

"How are we going to pay?" someone asked.

Desmond frowned, knowing this was a weak point in the plan. "As for credits, we have none. But jumping over the turnstiles is easy. Decker tells me there aren't any cameras or guards at the turnstiles."

"For those of you who are less agile, we can lift you over," said Decker.

"Let's do it," Bridget said. "It's a bold plan, and there's no way President Grieves would anticipate it."

Kate laughed. "I'd love to see the look on her face when she realizes what we did."

The groups settled down after a while. Decker knew they trusted both leaders, but it was still a dangerous plan. He hoped he wasn't being reckless. Or that their luck would run out.

When they neared the ITS station, Jeremy went ahead of the group to look for any sign of security squads, since it was possible that President Grieves had increased security at the station. Once he determined it was safe, the Dreamers entered the station, trying to look like they fit in. Decker wanted to tell them not to try so hard, but he admired how much they were working on looking like city dwellers.

After the last Dreamer jumped over the stile, they boarded two adjacent trains. Another attempt at looking like it was just any day in the life of a West City dweller. No one else boarded for several stops until they neared the city. When a family of Sleepless entered one of the Dreamers' train cars, Decker braced himself for a conflict. There was none. No one paid attention to them. They were too busy trying to keep their children in line.

In the Capital, some of the Dreamers who had never been there asked for a few minutes to look around. Against his better judgment, Decker agreed, although the thirty minutes he gave them felt like thirty hours. He watched them ride up the escalator like an excited bunch of tourists.

Everyone returned to the ITS, ready to board the second train to South City. They were amazed by how much nicer the Capital was than their home cities and told the Dreamers who weren't brave enough to venture out with them.

"This is going smoothly, Decker," said Kate. "This was a good idea."

"Congratulate me once we're off this train and in the woods again," he said, still nervous. "But I appreciate your faith in me, Katie girl."

Kate smiled and gave Decker a kiss on his cheek. His heart skipped a beat and he squeezed her hand. Maybe he'd find the guts soon to give her one in return. One on the lips.

Once outside the ITS station in South City, the Dreamers walked into the woods in high spirits. So far no one was following them, and they were hours away from finding a door out of their nightmare. Decker was so confident he started whistling, and others joined in.

"Decker," said Annie, "once we get to the Wall, we veer west for a little bit, and then we'll be at the door."

"How do we recognize the door? Is it hidden?" asked Kate.

"It has ivy all over it and a stack of old construction equipment in front of it. If you didn't know what to look for, you could easily miss it. We should be there in about two hours."

Arlene looked visibly excited. "If I'd heard rumors of a door, we would have searched."

"Yeah," said Desmond. "It kind of feels like we wasted so many years in here."

Arlene nodded sadly. "To think that there was a chance of freedom. It's unfortunate no wanderers passed on the story to us."

"No matter," said Kate. "Now we're all going to leave together. Maybe this is better. Perhaps we were meant to take this journey together."

"Although you've seen that Chicago still exists, I won't truly believe it until we step through the door," said Arlene. "It's possible what you saw was a projection or a hologram. What do you think, Decker?"

Decker shook his head. "No offense, but I think you have a vivid imagination. What we saw and heard was real."

Bridget nodded.

"The real question is why we were told it didn't exist," he said. "I'm also worried about what the people on the other side have been told about us. Who knows what's been said about those of us living in the Nation. Annie, can you tell us?"

The expression on Annie's face said a lot. "Well, the rest of the population thinks that you're all dead. Once you were herded into the Nation, the U.S. propaganda machine went into overdrive. They told the citizens you were all dead and that the land within the garbage wall was tainted. These lies kept curiosity seekers and investigators away. Only a handful of us knew the truth." She looked down and kicked a small rock into the bushes. "The truth cost me my marriage. My husband hated the fact that I couldn't tell him what was going on."

Everyone nodded, feeling awkward about Annie's little confession.

Then Decker laughed. "It's kinda funny when you think about it. They think we're dead, and we thought the same about them. We should probably come up with a game plan for once we get outside. The last thing I want is to get shot in Chicago."

No one said anything, and they walked on in sober silence.

"There it is! Oh, Decker, it's the door!" said Kate.

At Kate's words, everyone broke into a run toward the door, excited about escaping. It wasn't until they'd gotten closer that murmurs of confusion echoed through the group.

"It's been destroyed," said Annie, a confused look on her face. "Who would do this? I came through the door two weeks ago and it was fine."

"It's Grieves," said Jeremy as he tried to push on the door. "It has to be."

"She's chasing us," said Arlene. "She probably figured if she couldn't find us in the wild, she might as well destroy our way out."

Several of the Dreamers began to weep. Others looked defeated. Kate looked solemn.

"Well, it worked. What do we do now?" asked Kate.

"Don't get discouraged, Kate," said Decker as he put an arm around her. "President Grieves won this battle, but we still have a lot of fight left. We go on. I won't let us quit. If there's one door, there might be another."

Decker looked at Annie for confirmation of his theory.

She pursed her lips, thinking. “I’ve heard there is a second door, but I don’t know the exact location, only that it’s in East Sector.”

“Will your key card work on that one?”

“It should.”

“Then I think we should look for it. Hopefully your key card will work for it, and if not, we’ll have to think of something else.”

CHAPTER NINETEEN

They went back to the ITS station in South City, but this time when they reached the Capital, no one asked to do more sightseeing. Instead, they moved quickly to the train heading to East City. The Dreamers were quiet during the ride, each of them contemplating who knew what. This concerned Decker because the group hadn't ever been this quiet. He had to think of a way to rally them.

Once they were in the woods of East Sector, no one displayed signs of excitement. Kate looked defeated, walking with her head down. Annie looked anxious, hoping the door they were looking for was still in working order.

"Arlene, would you do me a favor, please?" asked Decker.

"What do you need?"

"Would you give Kate a pep talk for me? It would be more effective coming from someone other than me. I can tell she respects you. A few encouraging words could go a long way."

"Sure, Decker." She walked over to Kate, and they slowed down so they could be at the back of the group. Decker casually moved nearby so he could overhear their talk.

"Why the long face, Kate?" Arlene asked.

"What if this other door is destroyed, too? What do we do then? I pride myself on being an optimist, but seeing the door in South Sector was devastating. I can't seem to find a reason to keep going."

"Stop talking that way. Of course you need to keep trying. What about the rest of us? Are you giving up on us? If you stop trying, others will notice. Your lack of motivation will spread. We might as well turn ourselves in today. There are people here that love you, and they're worried about you."

"I know," Kate said.

"Do you think I've never been disappointed or had a setback in life?" she asked. She patted Kate on the back. "Perk up, young lady. Things have been worse, haven't they?"

"Yeah, they have," Kate said.

Decker was relieved to see Kate give Arlene a smile, glad that Arlene was getting an emotional reaction from her. Arlene was talking to Kate as if she were her mother. Something Kate needed. Something Kate had never had. After several more minutes of conversation, they embraced and then sped up.

"Hey, Decker!"

"Yeah?"

"Let's go to the Wall!"

When they found the east door, it was intact. The Dreamers broke out in a spontaneous celebration. Some danced, some sang, others laughed with joy. Decker didn't want to be a killjoy, but he knew time was still short, so he let them celebrate while he pulled Annie over to the door.

"Annie, would you please try your key card to open the door for us?" he asked.

Annie reached into her backpack and pulled out the card. She walked over to the door and slipped it in, but much to their disappointment, it didn't work. Annie turned back to the Dreamers with a disappointed look on her face.

"I'm sorry, my key card isn't working. They must be programmed to work in only one sector. So we need to figure out what the code is to use the keypad."

Decker looked at Jeremy. "Can we do it?"

Jeremy shook his head. "The number of combinations possible is in the millions, man. We could be here for months trying random combinations."

"Yeah, you're right," said Decker.

"I mean, if you do the math, assuming the key code is seven to ten numbers, it's incomprehensible," said Jeremy. "It could be anything. We don't know if it's a four-number code or one with a hundred numbers. There's no way of knowing."

"Then I suggest we think about what would be significant to people on the outside," said Desmond. "More specifically, to the people that put together the Nation. There must be something that has meaning to the designers."

"If you ask me, the number was probably chosen by President Grieves," said Kate. "She seems to love control and have her brand be a part of everything that goes on around here."

"So what are some things that are significant to her?" asked Arlene. "Does anyone know her birthday?"

No one did.

"What would be important to President Grieves other than her birthday?" said Bridget. "I don't know anything about her past life BIB. If she has children, where she was born. Without any of that, even this might prove too difficult."

The Dreamers began conversations amongst themselves, trying to come up with ideas. Then Jeremy stood up, looking excited. He ran over to Decker, practically jumping up and down.

"I'm so stupid, Decker! We have her tablet! I'm so used to not having one, I forgot about it. We can look up her birth date."

Jeremy began swiping at a furious rate, trying to find a biography on President Grieves.

"I found it," he said after a couple of minutes. "She was born on August 5, 2066. Let's give it a try. She's so self-centered it's as good a guess as any."

"Desmond, you do the honors," said Decker. "We can try the full birth date first, and then we'll try both the four-number year and then the last two numbers."

Desmond nodded, walked up to the door, brushed away the ivy covering the keypad, then began typing in the numbers of President Grieves's birth date. He began with the long version: 08052066. They all waited for the light to change color. It turned red. There were loud groans from the Dreamers.

"Don't get discouraged, everyone," said Decker. "We can't expect to get it on the first try. Go ahead, Desmond, try a shortened version."

This time Desmond typed in 080566. A moment passed, then a red light appeared. More groans. Desmond tried again, this time keying in 8566. Another red light. He knew there was one more combination of her birthday and tried that one. 852066. And the final disappointing red light.

"Well, we tried, Decker. Any other ideas?" asked Desmond.

"Everyone, I want you to sit down and focus," said Decker. "There's got to be something else we're missing. In addition to her own birthday, what else would be important to President Grieves?"

"Desmond, what about reversing the month and day?" asked Bridget.

"That's a great idea. Why don't you try it?"

Bridget walked up to the door, anxious that it still wouldn't open. She typed in 05082066. Instead of a red light, the keypad started to flash. Then a computerized voice said, "Too many attempts. The keyboard is locked down for one hour."

"Oh no!" said Bridget. "Ugh, it's my fault."

Desmond shook his head. "It would have locked down for any of us. Don't beat yourself up."

"Let's not panic," said Decker. "Everyone, we need to prepare ourselves in case she shows up before we figure this out. Start gathering rocks, sticks, anything we can use to defend ourselves."

"I'll get some of us to build something we can hide behind," said Desmond.

Dreamers pried garbage off the Wall and set up a barrier in front of the door. It was four feet high and ten feet long. Just enough coverage for them to seek protection if they needed it. They piled stones and sticks on the ground behind the barrier, readying themselves for a fight. No one wanted to be captured. Especially since they were so close to being free. They believed Jeremy would figure out the code to open the door to a new life for them.

Once the preparations were complete, they still had fifteen minutes before the keypad was reset. To calm everyone down, Decker started passing out EnUR-G bars. Eating would lead to talking, which would lighten the mood.

"What are you going to do when you get to Chicago, Aidan?" asked Kirsten.

"I suppose it depends on what you do." She smiled at that.

Decker and Kate were having their own conversation.

"Do you think there's any chance Moongie is still alive?"

Kate asked. "She'd be thirteen now. Cats live a long time. It's possible one of the hazmat teams took her. Or am I wishing for the impossible?"

"Anything is possible, Kate. I promise we'll look for her when we get home. I can't wait to have a Chicago Dog and go for a run at Lake Michigan. Paint again, have a regular life. I want to paint a portrait of you, Kate!"

"I just want a regular life. But there's something we have to do first."

"What's that?"

"We have to figure out why you sleep. It might help Annie cure the rest of us. I don't want to take Somnum the rest of my life. I want to fall asleep because of a boring movie, or because I worked too hard, or just out of plain old boredom. To fall asleep for no particular reason sounds divine to me."

"Sorry, I didn't think of that. Of course we're going to find out why we're different. I'll devote my life to that, and to you if you'll have me, Kate."

Kate stopped in her tracks. "Did you just propose to me, Decker?"

His face flushed. He'd surprised even himself. "I suppose I did. What do you say? We've known each other for ten years, we get along, and most importantly, I love you, Katie girl. I always have."

Kate's eyes teared up, and she leapt up and gave Decker a hug. And then she finally kissed him on the lips.

"So is that a yes?"

"Of course it is! But let's not tell anyone until we escape, okay? I want them to focus on getting out of here and not on us for now. As soon as we get to Chicago, we'll make an announcement."

"Even though I'd like to shout our news to the world, I'll do whatever you want." He grinned at her.

Just then, Jeremy yelled, “YES!” Everyone rushed over to him.

“I think I’ve solved the problem of the keypad. What is the most important date to all of us?”

“A birthday. But we already tried that,” said Aidan.

“What else? What defines who we are and where we live?”

“Just tell us,” said Desmond. “What is it?”

“Does the date September 6th mean anything to you, Desmond?”

“Of course it does. It was probably the worst day of my life. The same holds true for every one of us.”

“We already know President Grieves’s birthday doesn’t work. So how about the thing that defines what she does? I suggest the code is September 6, 2101. The day insomnolence began.”

Jeremy let that fact sink in.

“Oh my God!” said Decker. “I think you’re on to something, Jeremy! Now all we have to do is figure out what combination of those numbers to use. Who wants to try? The keypad should be ready in one minute.”

No one answered.

“Kate, why don’t you do it?”

Kate wasn’t sure she wanted the responsibility, but she went to the door anyway. Once the keypad was ready, she keyed in 09062101. Red light. Next, she tried 9601. Another red light. She had two more tries before the keypad locked her out. On her third try, she chose 962101. Red.

“Kate,” said Decker, “you have one more try. This is going to be the right combination. I can feel it.”

Kate took a deep breath and walked away from the door, straight into Decker’s arms. After a hug, she was ready to try one last combination. For her fourth try she typed in 090601.

The light turned green.

The lock clicked and the door began to open.

Then a gunshot whizzed past Kate's right ear and hit the keypad, destroying it. To Kate's horror, the door started swinging shut. Before the door could close, Kate stuck her foot in it, then quickly replaced it with a nearby rock. Then she dove for the barrier.

"Get down! Hurry! Get behind the barrier, everyone!" shouted Desmond.

CHAPTER TWENTY

"Why are you listening to Frank?" Grater asked. "We watched the door, and the Sleepers didn't show up. I'll bet they're going west or even north. It seems foolish to circle back."

"You never learn. Do not question my decisions, Sergeant."

"Yes, ma'am. We'll go wherever you ask. No more questions."

"Good."

Glynis was mad at herself for giving up too soon when they were at the east door earlier. If they'd missed the Sleepers, this error in judgement would fall squarely on her shoulders. She wouldn't be able to blame anyone else. But she would find a way.

Some days she missed the old Glynis. She wasn't always so mean. When she'd first taken the position of president of the Nation, her motivation was idealistic as well as ambitious. During those first few days of chaos, Glynis found out the horrible side effect suffered by those affected. Being unable to sleep without a chemical supplement had seemed cruel and sad to her. When the then U.S. President approached her about leading the new Nation, she'd accepted without reservation. Little did she know her term would stretch to ten years.

"We're getting closer, quiet down!" said Cramer.

She could always depend on Cramer to keep A Squad in line. D Squad was following his orders now, too.

"President Grieves, how would you like to proceed?"

"When we get closer, if they're there, I want us to find a good hiding spot and watch them for a while. Maybe they haven't noticed the door. Even if they have, they don't have a key card or the combination, so we'll have time to get in the best position to capture them. I'd prefer not to kill any of the Sleepers because I need to question them. Understood?"

"Yes, ma'am," said both sergeants.

After a long day of marching back to the east door, the sound of talking became louder as they approached. Glynis thought she recognized one of the voices, but then dismissed the thought.

"President Grieves, the Sleepers are within shooting distance. Shall I have the others spread out?" asked Sergeant Cramer.

"Yes, spread out, but stand down until you get my orders. Who is the best shot in your squad?'

"That would be me, ma'am."

"If that's the case, come back to me once the rest of them are settled in their positions. Now hurry up."

"Will do, President Grieves."

Everyone moved into position. Glynis got as close as she could without alerting the Sleepers of her presence. She asked Sergeant Cramer to fire a warning shot and destroy the keypad at the same time. Then she shouted a warning to the Sleepers.

"Halt! Step away from the door!"

Glynis saw the back of a woman. She looked familiar. She turned around.

"Is that you, Glynis? It's Annie Beaumont. There's no need to shoot at us. We're unarmed."

"If that's true, then come out where I can see you."

Annie stood up with her hands raised, an anxious smile on her face.

"Let them go, Glynis."

"Call me President Grieves!"

"Please let them go, President Grieves. They're harmless."

No one moved, waiting for President Grieves to decide their next step. Glynis fumed. What was Dr. Beaumont doing here? She was one of the reasons the damned Sleepless virus that caused her this ten-year headache existed. In an irrational moment, she wanted to see Annie suffer. To die. Not that her death would solve Glynis's problems, but it would make her feel better.

"Kill her, Sergeant Cramer. Do it now, while she's still standing there like a fool."

"But, ma'am, she's unarmed."

"Do you think I'm unaware of that fact, Sergeant?" she snapped.

Cramer lowered his weapon. "I'm sorry, President Grieves, but I cannot shoot an unarmed civilian. It goes against everything I believe in."

"Such dramatics," Glynis said, rolling her eyes. "Give me your gun. You are relieved of duty. Report to my office tomorrow, Sergeant Cramer. I'll deal with you then."

She'd lied about shooting a gun before. It was the first time she'd held one in her hand. Surprised at the weight of it, she used both hands to aim. But before firing, she wanted to increase her chances of killing Dr. Beaumont by luring her closer.

"Dr. Beaumont, come closer, and we'll discuss the terms of your surrender."

Annie looked back at Decker. Glynis could see him shaking his head. *Damn that meddler.* Glynis was out of patience. She fired at Dr. Beaumont. The bullet intended to go through her heart flew wide and instead went through her upper arm.

Damn it, I missed. She watched her target scream and then fall behind the barrier. *Maybe she'll bleed to death.*

"Get ready to move in and capture the rest of them," said President Grieves.

Before they could move, a hail of rocks flew into the woods, hitting some of the soldiers.

"What the hell was that?" asked Remus.

"Rocks!" yelled Sergeant Grater.

Glynis glared at the pathetic barrier they'd erected and dodged a stone that flew her way. She hadn't expected them to fight back. The president was used to the complacent Sleepless. Always tired, they only had enough energy to earn sleep, not to fight back or protest. It was why the Sleepers had to be stopped.

"Stop!" Grieves shouted. "Let's talk about this. Shooting Dr. Beaumont was an accident. One of my security squad got trigger happy. I promise he'll be taken care of. Let's solve this like adults."

"Why should we trust you?" yelled Decker. "How do we know you weren't intentionally trying to kill her? You worried she'd tell us the truth?"

While Decker was speaking, President Grieves motioned to the squads to get closer to the Sleepers.

"What truth? And who am I speaking to? You wouldn't be Decker, would you? The leader of your rebellious group?"

"Did that traitor Remus tell you about me? If so, you

know we're determined to find out what happened ten years ago."

"Decker, if you and the Sleepers surrender, I will promise you three things. I won't kill any of you. Dr. Beaumont will get the medical attention she needs for her accidental gunshot wound. And finally, I'll tell you all about the plague of insomnolence."

Glynis got her answer in the form of sharpened sticks hurled their way.

"Last chance, Decker. Stop trying to be a hero and think of the rest of your group."

"You're wrong about me, President Grieves," said Decker. "I don't want to be a hero. I want to do the right thing. And trusting you is not it."

Glynis was furious. Who did this guy think he was? She knew what he said was true, but to have it said to her in front of all these people was unforgivable.

"You've given me no choice, Decker." Then she muttered to herself, "You'll regret this."

Someone stood up, and Glynis wasn't sure if it was Decker. It was an older man who had his hands up.

"Are you Decker?" she asked. "I'm glad to see you've come to your senses."

She saw another pair of hands trying to drag the man down. And then she heard a voice say, "No! Desmond, are you crazy? Get down. I can't lose you again!"

But the man continued. "No, I'm not Decker. I'm the other leader of this group. We are the Dreamers, because we dream of a better tomorrow. But there can be no tomorrow without compromise. I have my own terms. You let the rest of the group go through the door to find whatever they find. Then I'll come quietly with, and you can do whatever you want with me."

"You think you're in a position to demand anything

from me? I've never even heard of you, Desmond," Grieves said, her voice dripping with disdain. "You may be co-leader, but I'm not accepting anything without both of you."

At that point Decker stood up. Glynis could see the resemblance and knew that somehow they were related to one another.

"Yes," said Decker. "I'll surrender, too, if you do what Desmond asked. If not, then we will fight you to the death."

Glynis turned to Sergeant Grater. "Whatever happens next, do not kill the leaders. I need them alive. You can injure them, but they have to be breathing. Understood?"

"Yes, ma'am."

"Remus, get over here. I want you to go over to them and try to convince them to surrender."

Remus nodded and walked out of the woods, nervous that he might be attacked by Decker but more scared of what President Grieves would do to him if he disobeyed.

"You!" Decker said, his face flashing with anger. "I'm surprised you have the guts to face us, you rat! It's because of you that Stephen is dead!"

Remus stopped; it was obvious he didn't know. Glynis cursed herself for not telling him about Stephen.

Remus seemed to regain his composure and continued toward Desmond and Decker, holding out his hands.

"I've made some mistakes, and I didn't think Stephen would be killed. I'm truly sorry for that. He was a good kid."

"Forget the fake apology," said Desmond. "Say what you need to say and then go back to your boss."

"Look, President Grieves doesn't issue empty threats. If you don't surrender in the next few minutes, she'll order the squads to attack you. This, whatever this is, isn't worth it. There isn't anything on the other side. Come back with us and live in the city. Forget about your little rebellion."

"Get out of our sight!" spat Decker. "I would rather die than live amongst you."

Remus shook his head and walked back to Glynis.

"You heard them. They're a stubborn bunch. Based on my experience of being their prisoner, I know he's telling the truth. He won't be surrendering to you."

"Then we go and kill them all. But remember, leave the leaders alive for questioning. I don't really care about the rest of them."

Glynis saw the way the squads looked at her and didn't care. If they wanted to think she was crazy, so be it.

Without warning, sharpened sticks began to fly again, some of them hitting their marks. Some of the men cried out. Then the sticks stopped.

"Go!" yelled Grieves. "Get those bastards now!"

They rushed out of the woods, guns drawn. Some carried metal batons to beat the Dreamers. All with the same intent: to kill the traitors.

The Dreamers were out of sticks, but they'd saved rocks for this next part of the fight. As the soldiers got about halfway to them, rocks began to fly once more. Some men were felled, others were slowed down.

"Keep going, you cowards! It's just rocks. Anyone who turns back will be arrested!"

At last they reached the barrier but were surprised to see only two men. Decker and Desmond were the only ones there.

"This is for Stephen," Decker threw a rock at Remus's face, splitting his lip.

Remus screamed. He touched his lip, and his fingers came away bloody.

"This is for my lip!" Remus hit Decker in the head with his baton. Decker fell over unconscious.

Desmond continued to throw rocks until five of the

soldiers jumped on him. Remus came over to him and knocked him out. He looked over at the door and saw that it was closed. The keypad was disabled from the earlier shot.

The rest of the Dreamers were on the other side. Remus paled.

"What's going on over there? Is it over?"

"Um, President Grieves, there were only two Sleepers here," said Sergeant Grater.

"What? How can that be?"

"The rest are gone. They made it through the door."

EPILOGUE

When the confrontation between President Grieves and the Dreamers started, Decker told Kate to get everyone through the door. He kept the president busy while Kate ushered the Dreamers out. She was too busy to look behind her, but she assumed Decker and Desmond were right behind her.

But then when she heard the door slam, she looked back and neither of them were there.

"No," she whispered. She ran back to the door and tried to open it, but it wouldn't budge. "Decker!" she screamed.

Someone pulled her back. "No! No! We can't leave them!" She turned and saw Bridget grasping her arm, tears rolling down her cheeks. Bridget shook her head and pulled Kate into a hug.

Kate couldn't believe what was going on. She and Decker had gotten engaged minutes ago. How could this be happening? She looked up at the Wall, tears flooding her eyes.

"We'll get them back, Kate," said Bridget.

Kate wiped her eyes angrily. "I know. We'll get them back.

And then we'll let the world know just who Glynis Grieves really is."

<<<<>>>>

ACKNOWLEDGMENTS

To Crystal Watanabe my editor. Thank you for helping me find the right words.

To Artie Cabrera my cover artist. Thank you for creating such an awesome cover.

ABOUT THE AUTHOR

I have been scribbling stories since I was a child and love to write Science Fiction, Magical Realism, and Modern Gothic.

My first memory of Science Fiction was watching the television show, "The Twilight Zone". That series messed with my mind! My imagination developed, helping me discover the lack of conventional boundaries in storytelling. Because my fiction is character driven, the focus of my stories tends to be about emotions, relationships, and society.

I live in the Pacific Northwest with my greatest fans: my husband Mark, twin sons Aidan and Jared, and three cats. When not writing, I love to travel, run, use the Oxford comma, and of course read!

Join my newsletter for updates on my new releases and special promotions.

http://www.dkcassidy.com/newsletter/

If you enjoyed The Dreamers, please consider leaving a review. Thank you.

www.dkcassidy.com